I0574300

I just needed a minute to get my head right.

Maybe two minutes.

Maybe a year.

I took a sip of my drink, then set it aside.

Then I saw her.

A young lady strolling alone at the edge of the water, her bare feet in the damp sand, waving crashing over her ankles.

Not anything unusual in itself.

Except that she was wearing a wedding dress.

BILLIONAIRE'S BAREFOOT BRIDE

ALSO BY KATHRYN KALEIGH

Contemporary Romance
The Worthington Family

Billionaire's Unexpected Landing

Billionaire's Accidental Girlfriend

Billionaire Fallen Angel

Billionaire's Secret Crush

Billionaire's Barefoot Bride

The Heart of Christmas

The Magic of Christmas

In a One Horse Open Sleigh

A Secret Royal Christmas

An Old-Fashioned Christmas

Second Chance Kisses

Second Chance Secrets

First Time Charm

Three Broken Rules

Second Chance Destiny

Unexpected Vows

Begin Again

Love Again

Falling Again

Just Stay

Just Chance

Just Believe

Just Us

Just Once

Just Happened

Just Maybe

Just Pretend

Just Because

BILLIONAIRE'S BAREFOOT BRIDE

THE WORTHINGTONS

KATHRYN KALEIGH

BILLIONAIRE'S BAREFOOT BRIDE

BONUS SHORT STORY — SPELLS AND OTHER USEFUL THINGS

UNEXPECTED VOWS PREVIEW

Copyright © 2023 by Kathryn Kaleigh

All rights reserved.

Written by Kathryn Kaleigh.

Published by KST Publishing, Inc., 2023

Cover by Skyhouse24Media

www.kathrynkaleigh.com

No part of this book may be reproduced in any form or by any electronic or mechanical means, including information storage and retrieval systems, without written permission from the author, except for the use of brief quotations in a book review.

This is a work of fiction. Any names, characters, places, or incidents are products of the author's imagination and used in a fictitious manner. Any resemblance to actual people, places, of events is purely coincidental or fictionalized.

To learn more about Kathryn Kaleigh, visit

www.kathrynkaleigh.com

Kathryn Kaleigh

PROLOGUE

Ophelia

September 8, 1900

Ophelia stood looking out from the second-floor window of her home toward the beach along the western coast of Galveston.

The house still hinted of the scent of fresh lumber, seasoned with the scent of seawater carried in on the steady breeze. The pale sea green paint on the walls was her personal favorite. It felt almost like bringing the sea inside.

Standing with the window open, soft white curtains fluttering on either side, she looked out toward that open sea. The sky was a beautiful splash of reds and golds illuminating the soft puffy clouds, all reflecting over the endless blue water until the two, the sky and the ocean, blurred together into one indistinguishable haze.

The clouds moved quickly across the sky, casting shapes in lines and swirls.

White-capped waves rolled in, one after the other, steadily

slamming into the shore, then pulling away to do it all over again. The waves came in rougher and stronger than the usual gentle waves of the gulf.

The setting sun stood poised to drop below the horizon, bringing darkness with it. If the clouds continued, there would be no moonlight to cast its glow upon the water. Instead, there would be utter darkness making it impossible to see across the water.

There was an energy in the air. An unusual electricity that made the little hairs at the back of her neck stand on end.

Ophelia was scheduled to leave Galveston in the morning to make the trip into Houston to stay with her sister for the next few months.

As far as her sister knew, Ophelia was going to Houston to await the return of her husband, Martinique. Martinique was stationed in the South African War and it had been five months since she'd seen him. For five months Ophelia had lived here in the house she and Martinique had built. Alone.

And that was an accurate assumption; however, Ophelia had an additional reason for wanting to spend the next few months with her sister.

Turning away from the window, she surveyed the half-empty trunks and boxes sitting around her bedroom.

She had until morning to get her belongings packed. Before the courier service would be here to pick everything up.

She had been putting it off. But it was time to just get it done now. Before nightfall. She didn't like wandering about the big house after dark. Instead, she stayed here in their bedroom.

Going to her bureau, she slid hangers along the bar, trying to decide which dresses to take with her. The problem was, she couldn't wear most of them. The question was would she ever fit into them again? Or would she be like her sister who got bigger with each of her five children, never returning to her pre-pregnancy weight?

She picked out three that were her favorites. With any luck, she would be able to wear them again.

After carefully folding them, she placed them in one of the trunks. Then knelt down and slid it across the wooden floor out of the way before it got too heavy for her to move.

Knowing better than to climb up on the footstool, she used an umbrella to slide her half a dozen hat boxes to the edge of the shelf where Martinique had put them. They fell noisily to the floor.

At least she would be able to wear her hats.

Drawn to the window and the ocean outside, she went back to look outside.

Dark clouds grazed the horizon. Storm clouds with lightning.

There was going to be a storm. A bad one.

There were things that needed to be done. Things that needed to be done to secure the house. Plywood over the windows. Other things she had no knowledge of.

She ran a hand along her stomach. She was six months along and in no position to do any of those things.

Today was the first day she'd felt like getting up and doing much of anything in ages. She'd felt so good, she'd sent the young lady who helped out during the days home early.

But the packing was turning out to be more overwhelming than she had expected. Everything was overwhelming these days.

She needed Martinique.

If he were here, he would know what to do to prepare for the storm.

1

CHRISTOPHER

I stood in the open doorway of the second-floor balcony of my rented beachfront cottage on a secluded section of Galveston Beach. Gentle white-capped waves slowly and steadily lapped at the soft sand as spindly legged white egrets picked their way along the shore.

Half a dozen noisy seagulls, squawking and mewing, coasted on the wind, some making dips into the water.

White puffy clouds—cumulus clouds—dotted the light blue sky. There was a hint of moisture in the air. The kind that only came from an impending storm.

Big ships drifted along the horizon, hazy, and looking like ghost ships. Closer in, two people on jet skis rode further out than I would have recommended. But I had a healthy respect for the ocean... and the sky. When man got off solid ground, man had to play by the rules of that world, whether sea or sky.

The soft, steady breeze coming off the beach carried the salty scent of the ocean with a slight but not unpleasant fishy smell.

It was four fifteen on an early October Saturday afternoon. Still hot compared to most of the country and the ocean water was still warm. Still attracting people to walk barefoot in the waves or inviting them to take a dip in the shallow water.

The beach was anything but crowded. I'd picked this secluded area of Galveston beach on purpose. To avoid crowds.

A man and his dog down a few yards to my right. Every time the man threw a stick into the water, the dog barked once and dashed into the water to fetch it. The dog would bring it back and they would do it all over again.

To my left I could see a carousel about a half mile or so down the beach along with the flashing lights of what looked like a county fair. When the wind was just right, the scent of corn dogs and cotton candy drifted this way along with the sounds of screaming children and discordant music from the rides.

Normal. It was so normal and serene it was almost painful to experience.

I sat down in one of the two wooden chaises on the balcony and put my feet up. I rested the glass of Crown Royal I held in my hand on my thigh. I hadn't touched it yet. Right now I was just enjoying the scent of it. The sight of the amber liquid swirling in my glass.

I had the cottage to myself for as long as I wanted it. And right now I had no idea just how long that would be.

I'd slept fitfully last night, my first night here, waking several times. Disoriented.

One time I thought I'd heard gunfire.

After walking downstairs and looking out all the window and doors, I decided it was just one of those nightmares.

Then finally about dawn, when the sun started coming up, I'd let the steady slosh of the waves lull me into a deep sleep. One of the deepest I'd had since Iraq.

Medals and honors of valor meant nothing here stateside.

A great blue heron flew past me, wings flapping noisily, heading for the water.

Two young men jogged along the beach, their indiscernible voices mixed with laughter floating on the breeze. They reminded me of where I had come from. Major. Special forces. Ten years. Early retirement.

Retired at thirty-two. Not what I had planned. Not how I had envisioned my life plan. Now I basically had to start my career over again. Figure out what I wanted to do next.

And I wasn't about to face my family without at least some idea what that direction might be. Otherwise they would decide for me.

The Worthington family had no lack of career possibilities.

I just needed a minute to get my head right.

Maybe two minutes.

Maybe a year.

I took a sip of my drink, then set it aside.

Then I saw her.

A young lady strolling alone at the edge of the water, her bare feet in the damp sand, waving crashing over her ankles.

Not anything unusual in itself.

Except that she was wearing a wedding dress.

2

———

ISLA DENTON

I sat on the bottom step of the little chapel only a few yards away from the water of Galveston Beach.

Sea gulls squawked as they flew in what looked like random nondirectional dips and swirls. Like my life. Just a series of random patternless motions. The more I tried to shift my life into some kind of order, the more out of control it seemed to get.

The ocean smelled like heaven. The Galveston beach held a magic for me. Fond memories starting with the first time I'd splashed into the waves on my father's shoulders at age three.

The county fair was within walking distance down the sandy beach to my left. Flashing lights and carnival music mixed with happy laughter and squeals. Fond memories there, too.

I took off my shoes and squished my toes in the sand, and looked toward the horizon. People frolicked in the water. On jet skis mostly.

They would be able to see dolphins this time of year. The dolphins would follow alongside the jet skis. It was a beautiful thing to experience. I often wondered whether the dolphins thought we were stupid for being out there or if maybe we were a rare kind of fish.

The wind shifted and brought a distinctive whiff of fried everything from the carnival.

"He'll be here," Momma said, standing behind me, but I could hear the nerves, the doubt, in her voice.

We both knew that Franklin Milton, III would not be showing up today.

Daddy was talking to the judge. Judge Peters was a personal friend of his. Daddy had paid him who knows how much to drive from Houston to Galveston for the afternoon.

Daddy wouldn't be mad about that. But he would be embarrassed. Daddy was easily embarrassed. I already knew what Momma would say. Momma would say it wasn't meant to be. That it wasn't in my cards or something of that nature.

Momma came and sat next to me. She was wearing a flowy flowery dress. She would have made a good hippie if she'd been born a little bit earlier. Grandma had been a hippie. God rest her soul.

It was funny. I'd been fine until I started thinking about Grandma. Now my eyes were filling with tears.

"I'm sorry, Momma," I said. "I need to take a walk."

I got up and walked straight to the edge of the beach. I didn't even look back.

I knew Franklin wasn't coming and they knew it.

As I reached the water lapping against the shore, I stopped and gazed toward the horizon—that hazy spot where the water and the sky blurred into one. The sun would be setting soon. It was going to be a beautiful sunset just like I'd known it would.

A beautiful sunset for wedding pictures.

I'd known. Didn't I? Surely there had been signs. There were always signs.

It didn't matter anyway.

The water splashing over my toes was cool at first, but I

knew it wouldn't take long to adjust and it would be comfortable.

I gathered up the full skirts of my wedding dress and took off walking along the edge of the water in the wet sand. My toes making little tracks one second and washed away the next.

I hadn't needed the fancy wedding dress with such a small wedding, but I'd had fun with it and I would have… would *have* had lovely wedding pictures. I even wore long, sheer gloves embellished with little sparkling crystals that came up over my elbows and the dress had a light blue sash around the waist.

This area of the beach was lined with cottages, some quaint, some fairly new. Some of them were people's homes and others were rentals. High priced rentals. A cottage painted in blue with wide steps that led down to the ground. A little two-story cottage with a wide balcony. No steps on the outside of this one.

I reached a man tossing a stick out in the water for his dog.

He nodded and went on his way as though women walked along the beach all the time in their wedding dresses. And I was sure they did. Just not alone.

The white fluffy clouds tossed around the light blue sky were beautiful, but they carried the harbinger of a storm.

There was a tropical storm out somewhere in the gulf, but they said it was a slow moving storm. Nothing to worry about and all that.

Still. I needed to head back. See about cleaning up the mess at the little chapel from the wedding that didn't happen.

Try to figure out the next step in my life without the man I was supposed to be married to by now.

I had so much to do thanks to Franklin and his vanishing act.

I turned my face up to the sun and let the wind tug my hair free from the clips. The calm before the storm. Just a few minutes more.

Not just the weather, but my life.

I had no doubt that unraveling a wedding that didn't happen was no less trouble than putting the thing together to start with.

I turned and started back the way I had come. The wind whipped at my skirts as I stepped over broken seashells and squished my toes in the mud. The tide was coming in. Slowly but surely.

As I walked by the cottage with the steps leading down to the beach, a man wearing shorts and a t-shirt, a baseball cap, was coming down them.

He was almost to the water just as I passed his cottage and he was looking at me curiously.

"Did you lose your way?" he asked.

3

______

CHRISTOPHER

I'd seen a lot of things during my military travels. A lot of things burned into my brain that I wish could be unburned.

But this was the first time I had encountered a beautiful bride walking along the beach, the ocean lapping at her toes. A beautiful bride walking alone.

Maybe it was the alone part that caught my attention. If she'd been with someone, anyone, I probably wouldn't have given her much more than a passing glance just as I did the man throwing the stick into the ocean for his big gangly black lab, not much more than a puppy.

But as it was, I felt obligated, as an American soldier—veteran now, but soldier at heart—to explore this situation further.

I was a sucker for a damsel in distress and a woman walking alone on the beach wearing a wedding dress seemed to fit that definition.

I walked slowly, watching her as she watched me. The closer I got to her, the prettier she got.

The wind had tugged her hair loose from whatever hairdo

she'd had. With a sister and a host of cousins, I was well schooled in what a wedding hairdo was supposed to look like.

It was not supposed to look like this. A bride walking alone down the practically deserted beach. Her hair tousled in the wind.

"Did you lose your way?"

"Maybe," she said, licking her perfectly bow-shaded lips and looked at me with emerald green eyes framed by thick lashes.

I'd reached the water now and was blocking her way. The only way around me was to go further into the water or walk around me in the loose sand on the other side.

The water lapped at my feet, soaking my old and battered white canvas sneakers I wore without socks. I wore a pair of khaki shorts and a t-shirt with an image of an American flag and USAF plastered across the front.

A flock of sea gulls squawked overhead, ignoring us. The egrets, however, had moved on to less populated areas.

"You seem a little overdressed," I said.

A hint of a smile touched those perfectly bow shaped lips and she shrugged. She looked up at me with those spellbinding wide green eyes.

"Change of plans," she said.

"So it seems. Can I walk you… wherever it is you're going?"

She shrugged and started walking again, forcing me to move aside unless I was willing to let her walk into me. That idea actually didn't seem so bad. As she moved close, I could smell her perfume. Magnolias. And a hint of peonies.

Her toenails matched her scent. A deep rose peony color.

"Suit yourself," she said.

I stepped aside and fell into step alongside her.

"It's a beautiful sunset," I said.

She cut her eyes at me.

"But you knew that," I said.

"I noticed."

We walked in silence. The rush of the waves splashing over our feet. My shoes, soaked now, squeaked as they squished out water with every step.

"You ruined your shoes," she said.

"They'll dry."

She slowed as we approached a little chapel, two men standing just outside the door.

"Is this you?" I asked.

"How did you guess?"

I smiled. I liked this girl.

This barefoot bride who wasn't a bride.

The girl with the long wind tousled hair. Perfect bow shaped lips. The green eyes of a siren.

4

ISLA

The little chapel had been in the perfect location. Just down from our summer cottage. Grandma and Grandpa had lived in the cottage full time when they had been alive. They had sold their house in Houston and moved to the beach. They loved every minute of it.

Now my family used it for our summer cottage.

"Is this you?" the man asked.

He was wearing a t-shirt with USAF and the image of an American flag on the front of it. His baseball cap had USAF on it, too. If I had to guess, I'd say he was an Air Force guy.

I looked over at the chapel. At Daddy and the Justice of the Peace. I could go over there, but I'd rather not. They would try to comfort me. Tell me everything was going to be okay.

"Nah," I said and kept walking.

The man, my new friend, didn't move at first, then quickly caught up.

I smiled to myself. It was a logical assumption that a girl wearing a wedding dress would be heading to a chapel.

Our cottage was just a little ways down. It was easy to spot as we neared. A couple of bunches of white helium balloons tied around the back porch posts, tossing in the sea swept breeze. My mother insisted that we do some kind of decorating even if it was just supposed to be Franklin and me , our parents, and my aunt.

Momma was like me. I had to have the dress and gloves and light blue sash tied around my waist. She had to have the balloons and cake and champagne.

I stopped in front of the house, letting the waves spill over my feet and splash water on the dress. Not that it mattered.

"Want some cake?" I asked, fully expecting the guy to turn around and head back the way he had come.

"Sure."

I shrugged and, dropping my skirts, let the hem drag in the sand in the back and began the walk up to the house. My mother would be there. And my aunt.

"There you are," Momma said as I came through the door.

Then she saw him.

"I brought a guest," I said, flopping very unladylike onto the sofa. Franklin would say I was not being proper. He concerned himself with such things.

"Hello," Momma said. "I'm Kate Denton. Isla's mother."

"Hello. I'm Christopher."

Momma glanced at me, then back at Christopher.

"Would you like some cake?" she asked.

"Absolutely," he said.

"Well," Momma said, narrowing her eyes at me. She didn't have to say it. She wanted to know why I had just left him standing there. "Come on in and have a seat. I'll get the cake."

I ignored Momma and pulled my phone out of my pocket. I should be given some leeway. I was, after all, the jilted bride. No messages or missed calls.

Christopher sat down on the other end of the sofa.

"How long have you known Isla?" Momma asked around the corner from the kitchen.

I looked at Christopher with one raised brow. Waiting to see what he was going to say.

"Not very long," he said.

"Well," Momma said. "I'm glad she ran into you." She came back carrying three pieces of what had to be wedding cake on a tray.

"Might as well eat it," she said. "No sense in it going to waste."

"I agree with that thinking." Christopher took a plate from her and handed it to me before taking one for himself.

"Where's Aunt Mae?" I asked and I set my untouched piece of cake on the end table.

"She's still at the chapel. Cleaning things up. You know her. She has to stay busy."

A loud noise came from overhead. It sounded like a stack of heavy boxes crashing onto the floor.

Christopher looked up toward the noise overhead.

"Is someone else here?" he asked.

"No," Momma said. "That's just Ophelia. Don't worry. She's harmless."

Christopher looked at Momma. Then at me.

"Ophelia lives here," I said.

"Oh. Well."

"Ophelia is a ghost."

5

CHRISTOPHER

I gave myself points for not reacting.

The crash of heavy boxes onto the floor above us was followed by the sound of one of those boxes being dragged across the room.

My appetite suddenly faded, I set my half-eaten piece of cake on the end table next to where I sat.

"What is she doing?" I asked.

Mrs. Denton shrugged and crossed her legs.

"Packing her things to leave."

"Why? Why would she be packing her things?"

"It's a long story," Isla said, pulling her feet up beneath her.

Another box landed on the floor.

"I'd like to hear it," I said. "But first do you mind if I go up and have a look? Just to be sure."

"Go ahead," Mrs. Denton said with a casual wave of her hand. "Put your mind at ease."

"I'll be right back," I said, wondering how I could possibly put my mind at ease when there was supposedly a ghost in the house.

Wary. Well aware that I was in a stranger's home. Also aware that I had no weapon, I made my way upstairs.

The cottage was open and airy. Central air conditioning blared inside the house, all the windows closed, keeping out the heat as well as any fresh ocean breeze.

Unlike my cottage, this one looked more like a home from what I'd seen so far anyway.

I reached the top of the stairs and, looking right, then left, decided to go right. That should put me right over the living room.

I knocked. Why, I don't know, on the first door to my right, then when there was no answer, I slowly pushed open the door.

There was no one there and there were no stacks of boxes. No boxes at all, in fact.

There was a queen-sized bed, neatly made up with a light blue comforter and matching pillow shams.

I looked in the closet, but the closest thing to a box was the empty suitcase.

I systematically made my way through the upstairs rooms, not finding anyone. No one named Ophelia and no boxes.

Perplexed now and not a little bit concerned, I went back downstairs.

The ladies were right where I had left them, seemingly unconcerned with a perfect stranger plundering through their home.

"I think you should call him," Mrs. Denton was saying to Isla.

"I'm not going to call him, Momma," Isla said. "He didn't show up. I think that's his way of dramatically saying he wants to break up."

"But what if he was in an accident."

"Someone would have called," Isla said.

Apparently, Isla had been left at the altar, but she was

remarkably unconcerned by it. She seemed more annoyed with the whole thing more than anything else.

When I stepped back into the living room, she was adjusting the long, embellished gloves she wore. I'd been to enough charity functions before being deployed that I'd seen fashionably dressed ladies wearing gloves before. But not long gloves that went up over the elbow. Must be the new fashion. A lot of things changed over the years.

I'd been home a few times, but not enough to keep up with ladies' fashion trends. Was it wrong that I was attracted to this woman who had almost married someone else today?

It was his loss, I decided. His loss and his stupidity.

"I'd like to hear the story about Ophelia now," I said.

6

ISLA

There was nothing Momma delighted in more than telling her great... great... great? Grandmother's story.

Before settling down to tell the story, she brought out the bottle of champagne that was supposed to be for celebrating my wedding.

I watched the amber liquid bubbling in my champagne flute as Momma settled in to tell the story.

"Ophelia lived here at the turn of the century. The nineteenth century. 1900. From all accounts, she was a young, happily married woman. She lived here alone while her husband fought in the war."

"Which war?" Christopher asked.

"I think it was the South African War. We don't know why." She waved a hand. "Anyway, back then they didn't have radar and all that for weather predictions."

"The 1900 hurricane," Christopher said.

"Yes," Momma said. "When the winds started and it was evident there was going to be a storm, she sent her sister who lived in Houston a letter. I think they had couriers then. But the letter told her sister that she was going to pack up her things and evacuate."

I adjusted my gloves. They were truly my favorite accessory. Christopher seemed to hang on every word of Ophelia's story. It was interesting, but I'd heard it a thousand times. Even told it myself.

"But the hurricane hit and she never got to leave here. Lost in the storm. We believe that she's still here, packing her things, trying to leave."

"That's a very sad story," Christopher said. "Very disturbing."

"It is, isn't it?" I said, turning to look at him.

His sparkling blue eyes met mine and I felt something shift deep inside me.

I'd been with Franklin for five years. It was difficult for me to say exactly what had attracted me to Franklin in the first place.

We just became comfortable. Then the pressure to get married started. I didn't really want to get married, nor did he.

But neither one of us could combat the pressure from our families. It was a subtle pressure. The kind that got under the skin like a splinter. The only solution to it seemed to be simply to get married.

So for the past five years, I had deprived myself of being attracted to anyone else.

And here, right here, on what was supposed to be my wedding day, I find a man that I could actually be attracted to.

Wasn't that how it went though? I'd always heard that, but I'd never actually believed it.

"How often does she... move boxes around?" Christopher asked.

"It varies," Momma said. "Mostly when there's a storm on the way."

All three of us pulled our phones and looked up the location of the storm in the gulf.

"They're showing it going toward Louisiana," I said.

"No," Christopher said "That's just one model." He glanced up, then back down at his phone. "The one I use has it coming straight for Galveston."

"Which one do you use?" I asked.

"It's just a private app," he said. "Pilots use it."

USAF. Pilots. He was most likely using a military app. Just didn't want to tell us.

I glanced up toward the ceiling where we'd heard Ophelia moving the boxes around.

Now I was a bit worried.

Ophelia just might be trying to tell us something.

"It's supposed to just be a tropical storm, right?" Momma asked, looking up at Christopher for confirmation. Momma had a tendency to overreact at times.

"I'm not sure they really know," he said.

"But they would tell us if we needed to evacuate, right?"

"Yes ma'am," he said. "I'm sure they would."

I wasn't so confident. And from the look on Momma's face, she wasn't either.

"I'll be in the kitchen," she said, gathering up the plates of uneaten cake without asking if we were finished. "Maybe I'll do some baking."

After she was in the kitchen, I turned to Christopher. "Do we need to evacuate?" I asked.

7

———

CHRISTOPHER

Isla's mother reminded me of a hippie, even though she wasn't old enough to have been one. Her chosen wedding attire had been a flowery, flowy dress that looked like something a woman would wear to the beach.

It would have fit the location and perhaps even been the kind of thing a person would wear to a wedding, but not this one. Her daughter's wedding dress was quite traditional. Quite elegant and lovely. I didn't get the disconnect, except that it was a very small wedding and it didn't appear that a lot of planning had gone into it. Maybe they had gone with an eclectic theme or maybe the wedding had been spur of the moment.

Still I couldn't help but wonder if maybe this had something to do with why Franklin, the missing groom, had changed his mind. A more orderly and traditional man might not be so amenable to a small, spontaneous wedding on the beach.

Not a good enough reason, I decided, maintaining my impression that Franklin was an idiot.

"Are you okay?" I asked, now that Isla and I were alone again.

"Yes," she said. "Oddly enough I am."

"You knew him well?" I asked. "The groom?"

She smiled at that. "Maybe not quite so well as I thought."

"People would say it's for the best," I said. "To find out now and all."

"You think?" she said on a little laugh. "Maybe a few months… years… earlier would have been better."

"You were together a long time?"

"Five years," she said, adjusting her gloves, then picking up her champagne glass and taking a sip.

"Five years is a long time. So you started dating him when you were like… fifteen?"

She laughed. "Close enough."

I swirled the champagne in my glass. Studied her a moment. I barely knew her. Just met her. I now knew that it only took a moment to fall head over heels with the most beautiful girl I had ever seen. And I didn't say that lightly. I had been all over the world. I'd met lots of women, but none of them gave me this kind of feeling. This certainty.

This sense of rightness.

A thump was followed by the sound of another box being dragged across the floor above us.

Both of us looked up, knowing we wouldn't see anything.

Knowing there was no one there.

Unless Ophelia counted. The ghost of Ophelia from 1900.

I would have to think about that later.

"Is your mother making brownies?" I asked, leaning over so maybe I could see into the kitchen.

"Probably," she said. Took a sip of her champagne. "You might not want to eat too many of them."

"Why not?"

She looked at me sideways. "Brownies."

"Oh." Realization dawned on the heels of surprise. "Brownies."

"Yeah. Momma is something of a free spirit."

I laughed. Somehow I had wandered into an intriguing family.

Voices drifted in from outside followed by stomping feet to get some of the sand off, then the door opened.

A woman who looked quite a bit like Kate Denton and one of the men who had been standing outside the chapel stepped inside and closed the door.

I stood up out of respect as they came inside.

The woman went straight to Isla, leaned over, and wrapped her arms around her.

"Are you okay?" she asked.

Isla nodded, but her eyes welled with tears.

"You're better off," she said, sternly. "Franklin wasn't worth your time."

"Now you tell me," Isla said as her aunt drew back.

"Wasn't certain," she said. "until now."

"Have we met?" Mr. Denton asked me. He was an average looking fellow. Average height. Average weight. Looked like he kept himself in shape and he appeared to be good natured. I immediately liked him.

"No, Sir," I said.

"Well, no matter," Mr. Denton said. "I haven't met all my daughter's friends. Were you here for the wedding?"

"I just came for the cake," I said.

Isla shot me a look. I just grinned.

"Well," Mr. Denton said. "It's just as well. I guess you know by now the wedding didn't happen."

"Yes sir," I said.

As the aunt joined the mother in the kitchen, Mr. Denton sat in an armchair across from me.

Isla didn't seem inclined to move from her spot on the sofa. She looked relaxed on the surface, but I could see the tension beneath it.

"You in the Air Force?" Mr. Denton asked.

8

—————

ISLA

I watched as my father sat down and held a conversation about the Air Force with the man I had picked up while I was walking on the beach. A neighbor. That's what he was. And I hadn't picked him up so much as he had followed me home.

He could be a summer renter, except it was October. Could still be a rental. Or he could live here. I wasn't here enough to know.

Besides, this part of the beach wasn't known for its neighborhood parties. Most people who came here enjoyed the seclusion of the uncrowded beach.

The little chapel had been here since I was a child, visiting my grandparents in the summers. It was just logical that I would want to get married in it.

Franklin certainly hadn't cared. That was probably the first sign that things weren't right.

A groom should care. A least a little. Right?

The companionable conversation between my mother and her sister drifted from the kitchen while Daddy and

Christopher talked about the Air Force, cars, and then their conversation turned to the weather.

I wasn't sure if I felt the hum of the impending storm or if the tension I felt was the result of my wedding falling through.

Either way, I was inclined to just sit here, calmly sipping my champagne, and letting my emotions settle. I had a feeling that if I did anything else, I might just shatter.

I couldn't explain why, but I liked having Christopher here. He looked like he belonged. Franklin had never looked comfortable here.

He'd always had a sense of impatience resonating off him. Like he couldn't get out of here quick enough.

An accountant in Houston working with his family's firm, he was finding less and less time for me.

He considered anything even resembling a leisure activity to be a waste of time. He never came right out and said so, but it wasn't hard to figure out.

Spending time with my family certainly wasn't a top priority for him.

I guess he couldn't find it in himself to drive down here to get married.

I wasn't mad about it though.

In fact, if I looked deep, I knew that I was relieved.

"Isla?" Daddy asked as though he'd been trying to get my attention.

I looked up to see that both men were watching me.

"Are you okay?" Daddy asked, a little frown creasing his brow.

"I'm fine, Daddy."

"Christopher tells me Ophelia is upstairs."

"The storm," I said with a nod. "I wonder if she'll ever find peace."

"I hope so," Daddy said.

"Okay," Momma said, coming out of the kitchen with a platter of brownies. "Brownies for everyone."

I shook my head as did Christopher.

"I'm going outside to watch the sunset," I said, pulling myself out of my stupor and standing up. "Want to come?" I asked Christopher.

"Sure."

As I headed out the back door, I wondered if I should probably change out of my wedding dress into something more appropriate, but I had grown rather fond of it.

I sat down on the porch swing, arranging my skirts around me.

Christopher sat down next to me.

"Thank you," I said.

"For what?"

For what indeed.

"For walking me home and keeping me from being alone."

"The pleasure was all mine," he said.

"I guess you can see my family is a bit eccentric."

"I find them quite entertaining."

"Not everyone does," I said, pulling my bare feet up and clasping my arms around my knees. Christopher gently rocked the swing.

The sun was starting its downward descent, getting ready to close down the day. A day I was happy to have behind me. Had I been looking forward to it? I didn't even know anymore.

The seagulls kept up their noisy, random flight path, dipping low, looking for food.

"You live here?" Christopher asked.

"No," I said. "I have an apartment in Houston."

"Your parents?"

"They have a house in Houston, too. My grandparents lived here for awhile, but it's our summer home now."

"It's nice," he said, not volunteering anything about himself.

"What about you?" I asked. "You live here?"

"It's a rental."

"Where do you live?"

He gazed out across the ocean where the steady lap of the water gently kicked at the sand.

"I'm currently in transition," he said.

"Well," I said. "You have to be *from* somewhere. Everyone is from somewhere."

"Military," he said, touching the brim of his hat.

"Well, you weren't born in the military."

"Good point," he said. "Houston. Born and bred."

9

———

CHRISTOPHER

When Isla was called inside to talk with her brother on a phone call, I told her I would see her later and left her house.

It was odd. I felt perfectly comfortable there with this bride who wasn't a bride that I had literally just met.

But she had things to do and I was comfortable intruding only just so much.

Besides, her family was having brownies. Brownies that undoubtedly had a little something special in them.

Couldn't blame them. Their daughter had just been jilted at the altar.

No one seemed especially distraught over it. Isla seemed a bit stunned, but not upset.

As I walked back, following the shoreline back to my own cottage, the sunset blossomed into a splash of pinks and oranges. If I had any artistic talent at all, I would capture this view on canvas.

But artistic talent didn't run in my family. We had pilots and psychologists, mostly. A couple of engineers and a healthy dose of entrepreneurship mixed in. I was the only one who had attempted to make a career out of the military. My mother had spent some time in the service and I figured I took after her.

The wind was picking up and by morning I suspected there would be clouds where there was sunshine now.

I walked up my steps and mentally kicked myself. I'd been planning on spending the foreseeable future here in my cottage. Alone.

Giving myself time to reflect and get myself mentally prepared to face my family.

Instead, I'd gone and distracted myself by a beautiful woman walking alone along the beach in a wedding dress. Maybe there was something about a wedding dress that intuitively drew a person's attention. Much like a baby's cry. Something that called on us to pay attention.

I didn't know anyone, man or woman, who could walk past a bride and not look. It was just a thing.

This was, at least, what I told myself.

Anything else would be absolutely insane.

I'd followed the girl home, for God's sake. Had champagne with her and her family.

And learned about the ghost of Ophelia.

Not exactly a run of the mill encounter.

I'd heard the boxes falling and scraping along the floor myself. But there had been no one upstairs. I had looked myself.

And, I opened my weather app while I sat down on the chaise, there was a storm coming.

And from the looks of my weather app, it was going to be here sooner than the main stream forecasters predicted.

With my grandfather being the founder and owner of Skye Travels, the largest private aviation company in the country, I had access to the best weather apps. And if that wasn't enough, I had my military weather app.

The military had access to information other people didn't have and as an honorably discharged veteran, I still had access.

Tomorrow I would evacuate. I wouldn't put myself in a position to end up like Ophelia.

But, before I left here, I would warn the Denton family. Tell them what I knew. To give them a fair chance at getting out too before evacuations were ordered and the freeway out of here got congested.

It would give me an excuse to see Isla again. To see if my attraction to her had been nothing more than a fleeting, passing thing.

I knew it wasn't, but I'd give myself forever to figure it out.

10

ISLA

From the sound of things downstairs, no one would have known that there had been no wedding. My parents and my aunt had imbibed on the brownies and were having a grand time.

I didn't mind. My aunt had flown in from Pittsburgh and hadn't been home in years. She and Momma were close. This was good for them.

I stood at the window and looked out toward the ocean. There were some stars visible, here and there. That meant that there were also clouds.

There was a tropical storm on the way.

Tomorrow, I decided, after I slept late, I would drive home. I would encourage my family to do so, too, but they could just as well choose to stay behind. Take some time to board up the windows. They had a good supply of plywood in the storage shed out back.

The only problem with my plan was not seeing Christopher again.

He'd followed me home like a stray puppy, an analogy I was

certain he wouldn't like. But it made me smile and right now that was hard to do so I would take it.

I looked around the room and shivered. My room was right over the living room. I was standing right where Ophelia would have been.

I had never been afraid of her. But the idea of ghosts had been a part of my life for as long as I could remember. I accepted it and went on.

Still. It was a little disconcerting to think that she had been here in this room. Packing her things. Getting ready to leave. Thinking she had plenty of time, only to find out too late that she had not had plenty of time.

The city had been destroyed.

Thinking about it terrified me.

Yes. I'd head out tomorrow.

Maybe I'd take a walk on the beach first, though. Just to see if Christopher would join me again. And if he didn't? Maybe I'd just waltz up to his door. He'd done basically the same.

As I stared out into the night, watching as clouds moved over to block the moon, I thought about Christopher. Wondered about him.

Wondered what it would have been like if he'd been the man I'd been waiting for at the chapel instead of Franklin.

Since I'd probably never see him again, I allowed myself to imagine what it could have been like.

Pressing a hand against my lips, I allowed myself to imagine his kiss.

I was a single woman again and, besides, there was no law against dreaming.

Christopher…

I didn't even know his last name.

Seeing him again was becoming less and less of a probability.

They would say it was the rebound effect. That when

Franklin hadn't shown up, I needed someone to take his place in my heart. To fill the hole so it wouldn't hurt so bad while I healed. And they would probably be right.

But I didn't believe it. I didn't believe that he was a rebound.

A rebound would have meant I had loved Franklin.

And the way I was feeling right now, I knew that it had been a very, very long time since I had felt anything for Franklin.

And with the way I was thinking about Christopher, I was beginning to doubt that I had ever felt much more than basic affection for Franklin. I wasn't sure what that said about me as a person since I had been about to marry him, but I suppose it was something along the lines of what my aunt had said.

I hadn't been certain.

11

CHRISTOPHER

The next morning all hell broke loose.

The sun's light was no more than just touching the edges of the horizon. A gentle breeze coming off the ocean brought the steady sound of water lapping at the sandy beach.

I'd been sleeping like the dead. A sleep without nightmares. One of those rare peaceful nights. Wasn't that just the way it went?

The first thing that happened was I got an emergency alert on my phone. I think I must have jumped straight up out of bed, it was so loud and intrusive.

My head still foggy from sleep, I sat up and blinked until I could read the message.

The West Beach bridge was out.

The West Beach bridge that connected this part of the island to the main Galveston island.

Out. How could the bridge be out?

I'd just driven it two days ago. It had been fine.

By the time I dragged myself into the kitchen and got a pot of coffee going, my phone started blowing up with weather alerts.

Overnight, the tropical storm in the gulf had strengthened to a category two and it was expected to strengthen to a category four.

While I waited for the coffee to brew, I went outside and stared out at the ocean.

Other than being a little cloudy, it looked normal to me.

But I knew better. A storm brewed in the gulf.

I made myself a cup of coffee and went back out to sit on the chaise to watch the sun come up.

This must have been what it had been like for Ophelia and all the others who lived in Galveston in 1900. They no doubt knew there was a storm coming, but they had no idea just how much of a storm. The hurricane that would change their lives as they knew it.

I did a quick google search. More than eight thousand people died in what they called the Great Galveston hurricane. One of the deadliest natural disasters in U.S. history.

Good God.

And here we sat. On the west side of Galveston with no way to evacuate. Not with the bridge out.

Whether it was 1900 or over a century later didn't matter when there was a storm of that magnitude bearing down on us and us having no way to escape.

As I sat there, I realized I wasn't just thinking of myself and all the other people who were stranded here. I was specifically thinking about Isla.

She was stuck here, too.

There was no airport on this side of the bridge. So having my grandfather send a plane to get us wasn't possible. Not even an option.

There were ferries though. There had to be ferries.

Another google search and I was no longer quite so certain.

The ferries were on the other side of the bridge.

I checked the weather again.

There was plenty of time to evacuate. The storm was still forty-eight hours out.

That put the storm making landfall sometime Tuesday if it continued on its current trajectory.

I refilled my coffee cup and watched the waves coming in. The back of my neck tingled. Just like it did before I went into any kind of battle.

It was a dangerous situation I found myself in.

I had to get both myself and Isla out of here. And her family. A girl like that wouldn't leave without her family.

I had some investigating to do. Then I had some phone calls to make.

I hadn't even told my family that I was stateside.

My parents wouldn't be happy, but it was my grandparents I really dreaded telling.

Grandma Savannah and I were close. She was the one I'd stayed in touch with the most over the years. She would have expected for me to at least have the courtesy to let her know I was this close to home.

And now it looked like I was going to be calling them for help.

12

ISLA

Chaotic. That was how I would describe the morning.

My phone alert had gone off, waking me out of a perfectly good sleep. And I'd heard the alert going off on everyone else's phones, too, all down the hallway. Momma and Daddy and Aunt Mae. Everyone would be up now.

Wearing my pajamas, I went out into the hall. Aunt Mae came out, wearing a long silky robe.

"The bridge is out," she said, looking at me, then back down at her phone.

"How can the bridge be out?" I asked, reading the alert again, then dropping my phone down to my side, looked at her for answers.

"I don't know," she said.

"Has this ever happened before?"

"Not that I know of."

Daddy stepped out of their bedroom.

"The bridge is out," he said.

Aunt Mae and I looked at each other.

"I've never known it to be out before," Aunt Mae said.

"Well, you lived here longer than any of us," Daddy said. "What are we supposed to do now?"

"You're asking the wrong person," Aunt Mae said. "I don't know."

Then our phones went off again. This time with a weather alert.

Momma came out, also wearing a long, flowing robe.

"I'll go make coffee," she said. "Looks like it's going to be a long day."

With nothing else to do, we all followed her downstairs.

I went outside and stared at the horizon where the early morning glow of the sun was just brightening that area where the sky and the ocean blurred together in one hazy line.

There was an energy in the air. A foreboding energy that I'd never felt here on the island. The island had always been a safe, calm place.

Daddy came outside, bringing two cups of coffee. Handed one to me.

The crash of boxes echoed through the house.

Ophelia was serious about packing her things and getting out of here.

"It's too late," I murmured.

"Don't tell her that," Daddy said, under his breath.

"What are we supposed to do?" The scent of the ocean was fishy this morning. Fishy and salty.

"I don't know yet," Daddy said.

"We have to do something," I said as Ophelia dragged a box along the floor in what was now my room. I looked down at my weather app again. Then looked up at Daddy.

"They're predicting it to become a major hurricane," I said. "Daddy. We're stranded here. Just like Ophelia."

"No," Daddy said. "We have an advantage."

"What?"

"We know it's coming. She didn't."

"But we're stuck here. Just like she was."

It was fate. Fate had brought us here for a wedding that hadn't happened. And now history was repeating itself.

Walking to the edge of the porch, I looked one way, then the other. There were no people out walking this morning. No dogs diving into the water after sticks.

No handsome men in sight.

I couldn't exactly walk past his house now. Not wearing my pajamas.

"Maybe there's a ferry," Daddy said.

"Maybe." We should know this kind of thing. People who lived on the island would know. Summer residents should know. Since we owned a home here, we, especially, should know.

Another box crashed onto the floor overhead.

I'd never heard Ophelia being so active.

This was not a good sign.

I was thinking about going back inside, getting dressed, when Daddy gestured with his coffee cup. "Your boy's coming this way," he said.

"Not my boy," I said, but my heart was beating too fast not to mean something.

13
___

CHRISTOPHER

The sun came up like it always did and it promised to be a beautiful Fall day on the beach. The seagulls had yet to leave the area ahead of the storm, so without my phone, I wouldn't have had any reason to suspect any particularly bad weather. And if I hadn't seen the forecast, I probably would have ignored the electrical energy in the air that stabbed through me like hundreds of tiny needles.

It hadn't taken long to find out that the island on this side of the West Beach Bridge was not only ultra-private, but it was also ultra-isolated. Made sense. One rather came with the other.

I made some calls and learned that the bridge was supposed to be back in commission by the end of the week. Unfortunately, with the current forecast, the repairs had been put off indefinitely.

I was told they would get on it as soon as weather permitted.

That was the whole problem. By the time weather permitted, it would be too late.

There were probably at least two dozen families stranded

out here. And that was just my guess. I didn't know the actual count. Had no way of knowing and until now no reason to know.

I had one more call to make. Two more counting my grandfather, but I was only going to call Grandpa Noah as a last resort. Since there was no place to land a plane on this strip of island, he couldn't help.

But my buddy could. My buddy was in the national guard now and he would have resources.

I paced along my porch while I called and left a message.

The timing was really bad. The national guard would be preparing for the hurricane. They just needed to add rescuing some people off a little isolated strip of island.

After I left a message, I put on a dry pair of shoes, packed all my belongings in my overnight bag—the only one I had—tossed it over my shoulder and headed down to the water. With the bridge out, my rented SUV wasn't going to do anyone any good.

I'd follow the beach until I reached the Denton's house. Then I would decide what to do from there.

As I walked just along the edge of the waves crashing onto the shore, listening to the calls of the seagulls, I already knew, not only where I was headed, but what I was going to do.

I was going to see Isla. Since I couldn't stop thinking about her, it seemed I had no choice but to go back to where she was.

And after that, I had no clue. One thing at the time. That was something the Air Force had taught me. Gather your facts. Go with your gut. Don't rush headlong into anything. Don't hesitate when the time was right.

Seemingly contradictory rules of thumb. But when they were put all together, they made perfect sense.

When I reached the Denton's cottage, the first thing I noticed was that the balloons tied around the porch posts were gone.

So the wedding celebration was officially over. I took that as a good sign, even though it had nothing to do with me.

Hoisting my overnight bag as I straightened my shoulders, I headed up the path toward the cottage.

They would have gotten the same alert about the bridge and the same weather alerts. So I wasn't telling them anything they didn't know.

But I could give them hope that there was a way out of this.

Besides, I couldn't bear the thought of leaving here without Isla.

It just wasn't going to happen.

That much I had already decided.

14

ISLA

I sat in the swing and waited until Christopher, my boy, as Daddy had called him, and really it was about the best way to describe him. Not that I particularly minded.

He was handsome and in a different way from Franklin. Franklin was most at home in a business suit, haircuts every week.

Christopher was handsome in a more rugged way. His dark hair just barely swept the collar of his t-shirt and his baseball cap gave him a slightly bad boy look that I hadn't known I was attracted to. He was wearing jeans this morning with a white t-shirt.

After Daddy had pointed out that Christopher was walking this way, I rushed upstairs and got dressed in record time. Just jeans and a light blue t-shirt. No shoes. I guess I was still showing off my prewedding pedicure.

I stood up as he started up the stairs and knew the moment he saw me.

He stopped and met my gaze.

His eyes, blue as a summer sky, held mine and I found myself smiling.

I was happy to see him. Surprisingly so. I'd been thinking about him since yesterday, but seeing him again let loose butterflies in my stomach.

It had been a long time since I'd had butterflies.

Too long.

And to think that I had almost married Franklin yesterday.

I shook off the thought.

"You're back," I said.

"Seems we have a problem." He made it to the top step. Leaned against the post. "Thought we might could find a way to solve it together."

"The bridge is out," I said. "And the storm is a hurricane now."

"So they say."

"Ophelia is inclined agree."

Christopher nodded and on cue, a stack of boxes crashed onto the floor overhead.

"She seems a bit upset," he said.

"Sensitive to storms."

"I bet."

I went back to the swing and sat down. He sat down next to me.

"Do you have more information?" I asked. "Than what came through on the alert?"

"Only that we have to find another way off this island."

The little spurt of panic was followed by relief that he was here. I felt safer with Christopher here. Not that he could do anything. But I had faith that he would figure something out.

It was his confidence, I decided. His confidence comforted me.

"Oh. Hi," Momma said, coming out the door and seeing Christopher sitting next to me.

"Hi," he said.

"Have you eaten?" Momma asked.

"Not yet," he said. "Sorry to intrude again."

"Nonsense," Momma said. "Don't apologize. I'll warn you though. Since you're here, we're likely to put you to work."

"I've never been afraid of work," he said. "But it sounds like Ophelia's already on top of it."

Momma laughed. "Come in here," she said. "Both of you. I made breakfast. Then we need to make some decisions."

15

CHRISTOPHER

"Old man Turner used to have a yacht," Aunt Mae said, filling a pitcher with orange juice and setting it on the table.

"A lot people used to have boats," Mr. Denton said. "But the HOA doesn't allow us to dock them anymore. The dock is on the other side of the bridge."

I hadn't thought about private boats. We could leave our cars here with private boats, unlike trying to take them on a ferry. It might be an easier thing to set up.

I sat next to Isla at the kitchen table. Her mother and aunt were still busy getting breakfast ready. Mr. Denton sat on the other end of the table, drinking coffee.

"We could call someone, get them to bring a boat over to get us," Mrs. Denton said.

"I think we should wait," Aunt Mae said. "See if it turns. The forecasters get it wrong a lot of times."

Boxes fell overhead, followed the sound of one being dragged across the floor.

"I don't think Ophelia likes that idea," Isla said.

No one said anything as boxes fell and slid across the floor.

I wanted to go look again. To see if maybe I had missed anything, but these people lived here, at least some of the time, and they acted like it was just a normal thing to have a ghost in the house making noise.

"Fine," Aunt Mae said. "Do you know anybody to call?" She pointedly looked at Mr. Denton.

"Don't look at me," he said. "We're hardly ever here anymore. It's not like we know a lot of people."

Mrs. Denton set a platter of food on the table. A plate of bacon. Eggs. Buttered toast.

"I hated for all this food to go to waste," she said. "At least we get to enjoy some of it." She sat down next to her husband.

"This is very nice," Aunt Mae said. "You know you didn't have to do all this."

I sat back and watched as everyone filled their plates. I'd missed this, I suddenly realized. This easy, comfortable family time.

I was the youngest of five, but we were all fairly close in age. The next oldest were twins. And there were always cousins around. The Worthington family was large and we were close.

And now, seeing the Denton family, as small as they were, actually made me homesick. I'd barely been home since I'd turned eighteen and this was the first time I could remember being homesick.

Everyone kept their phones out while we ate breakfast.

"We normally aren't this rude," Mrs. Denton said. "But it seems prudent to keep an eye on the weather."

I held up my phone. "I agree completely," I said.

"Do you have any ideas?" Mr. Denton asked me.

I liked him. He seemed like an amicable man and didn't appear to have anything to prove. Hadn't been a lot of people like him in the military. My best friend excluded.

Unfortunately that best friend had been injured, discharged, and sent home to Boston. That had been three years ago. And, although I still considered him one of my closest friends, we rarely talked anymore.

"I'm working on it," I said as they all looked at me. "I have a friend in the National Guard."

"Thank God," Aunt Mae said. "We'll be alright then."

Isla had her phone out again. "Maybe," she said, looking up at us. "They just deployed the National Guard to Louisiana."

"What?" Mrs. Denton said, looking from Isla to her husband to me. "What does that mean? Does it mean the storm is changing course?"

"No," I said, looking at my military app. "It's not. But the mainstream weather broadcaster seems to think it… might."

16

ISLA

*N*obody said anything. A gust of wind swept at one of the palm trees outside the kitchen window, brushing branches against the glass. A harbinger of things to come.

We'd finished eating breakfast. Momma had been right. We'd had lots of food that didn't need to go to waste. But now the breakfast I'd eaten sat heavy in my stomach.

The forecasters were telling the people one thing while they were sending the guard to do another.

"That doesn't make any sense," I said.

"Why would they do that?" Aunt Mae said.

"It has to be a miscommunication," Daddy said.

But we were all looking to Christopher for answers.

At the moment, he didn't appear to have any. He shook his head.

"I wish I knew the answer," he said.

"Don't you have connections?" Daddy asked. "With the Air Force?"

"We don't have a lot of connections after we go through discharge."

"Well," Aunt Mae said, standing up. "I'm going to call the police. See what they intend to do about this."

I agreed with Aunt Mae. Surely they were going to do something. There were people on this other side of the bridge. They wouldn't just leave us stranded. But if they thought the storm was going east...

"I'm waiting for a call," Christopher said. "From my friend."

Aunt Mae went off to make her phone call. Momma and Daddy went into the living room, probably to discuss options, leaving me and Christopher alone.

"Don't worry," he said. "I will get us off this island before the hurricane hits."

A box fell overhead and started sliding across the floor.

We looked at each other.

"I'll find a way," he said.

"I believe you," I said, realizing that I did.

The sliding stopped and there was silence above us.

I let my breath out slowly. Christopher had shown up in my life just at the time I needed him. Maybe it was fate.

Maybe he was an angel.

I tilted my head to the side and studied him.

"Why are you looking at me like that?" he asked.

"Just wondering if you're an angel."

He laughed. "Hardly. Don't ever confuse me for an angel. You might recall I was in the military."

I smiled a slow smile.

That would be hard to forget with him wearing his USAF baseball cap and looking quite sexy while doing so.

"I haven't forgotten," I said.

An alarm on his phone went off.

I stared at mine, but I didn't get it.

"Is that one of those military weather alarms?"

"Actually," he said. "Yes."

"Well," I said. "What does it say?"

17

CHRISTOPHER

*E*ither something was going on with the communication system or something was going on with the weather.

According to this latest report, the hurricane had weakened and shifted its trajectory to, just as Isla had said, Louisiana.

Her parents and her aunt had taken themselves off to other parts of the house, leaving me alone with Isla.

She started gathering up the dirty dishes and taking them to the sink.

I got up and scraped food into the trash, while she ran hot water into the sink.

I didn't see a dishwasher, so I it looked we were going to do dishes the old fashioned way.

It was hard to complain, though, when the view out the kitchen window was straight out over the ocean.

There were people walking along the beach now. Despite the weather warnings, everyone seemed to be doing whatever they wanted to do.

Normal things. Jogging. Swimming. Sunning.

"I'll wash," I said. "You dry."

"I don't mind—"

"I won't have you ruining your hands when I'm standing right here.

She shrugged and picked up a drying towel.

"Don't they know there's a storm coming?" I asked.

"They do," she said. "these are tourists. Right now they don't have anything to worry about. Besides. Where would they go? The bridge is out."

"True."

But it made little sense to me. People made little sense to me sometimes. Maybe I was overreacting.

Maybe the storm would go east and we would have worried for nothing.

"Does anyone know what really happened to Ophelia?" I asked.

"What do you mean?"

"Well, if she didn't have children, how are you her descendants?"

"Her sister and her brother came here afterwards. After the hurricane. Cleaned things up."

"I see. Which one stayed? The brother or the sister?"

"Neither." She took a plate, dried it and put it away. Then waited patiently for the next one.

"It was her niece who took an interest in the house."

"Huh." I handed her another plate.

"They say that neither her sister nor her brother could stand it here after what happened to their sister."

"That's understandable."

"I think so, too. Do you really think we'll get off this island in time?"

"I plan to do everything in my power to make sure we do."

"And if we don't?" she asked, looking at me with those startlingly clear green eyes. It was eyes like that that could lure a man onto the dangerous rocks.

18

ISLA

It seemed a bit hypocritical and maybe even a bit crazy at first, but after all the dishes were put away, Christopher and I went for a walk along the sandy beach. The sun had burned off any morning dew, but the air was still cool enough to be pleasing.

The water rhythmically lapped along the shoreline bringing a sereneness along with it that masked the churning storm in the gulf.

It was a beautiful day.

"Ophelia wouldn't have known," I said. "It would have been just like this, wouldn't it?"

"I would think so." Christopher stopped to pick up a seashell. Turned it over, then tossed it back into the sea so it could wash up again.

"It's scary."

"It is."

"We're so lucky we have technology," I said.

"Agreed."

I looked over at him with a little smile.

"You don't say much, do you?"

"Only when I have something to say."

Strong silent type. I never would have thought that was my type. I didn't really have a type and never really believed in the concept. I always figured love was something that would happen when it happened.

It would be one of those things a person had no control over.

And right about now, I was thinking I was right.

"Over eight thousand people died in that storm," he said, bringing my thoughts off of him and back onto the situation at hand.

"It's incomprehensible." I stopped and turned to face away from the water. Swept my gaze over the little cottages, some white, some painted in bright colors—blue, yellow, green, here and there, down to the carousel that sat idle. If the carnival was closed, this weather situation really was serious.

"It was a tragedy."

"We're lucky," I said. But what I didn't allow myself to say was that we might be very unlucky if we didn't get off this island before much longer.

The guy with the big black lab was up walking ahead. Tossing the stick along the shore, though, instead of into the water. The dog dashed forward, grabbed the stick in his mouth, and tail wagging, carried it back to the man.

The water was getting a little rougher and I hadn't even really noticed it until now. Good reason to keep the dog out of the water.

"I'm worried," I said, looking over at Christopher.

"You should be," he said.

"That isn't very comforting."

He started walking again, not saying anything.

"I thought you said we'd get off this island."

"We will. But it's still reason to worry."

We stopped again and faced each other.

He swept a lock of hair out of my eyes.

"Whatever happens," he said. "You can know one thing for certain. I am not leaving here without you. And since I know you won't be leaving here without your family, I'll be finding transportation for five."

19

———

CHRISTOPHER

*I*sla was looking at me with eyes bright with moisture.

My instinct was to pull her into my arms to comfort her.

I meant what I said. I wasn't leaving this island without Isla.

I was also planning, but it didn't seem like the right time to tell her, not to leave this island without kissing her.

The wind tousled her hair, making her even more beautiful, if that was possible, than she had been yesterday. Unlike yesterday's wedding dress, today she was wearing blue jeans and a t-shirt, much as I was.

But I'd noticed the way she filled out her jeans. To be such a little thing, she had quite the figure.

I stuck my hands in my back pockets to keep them off her.

"Thank you," she said.

It wasn't just that I would do anything to keep this girl safe, I'd do just about anything to keep from disappointing her.

I could get us out of here. I was certain of it.

I had an ace up my sleeve. All I had to do was to call my family, probably my grandfather, and he would have us out of here. The problem was, I had neglected my family for so long it just didn't seem right to call on them now that I needed them.

But I would. And they would help me.

When Isla tilted her face up to mine, her eyes drifting closed, any lingering reluctance I was having vanished.

She was inviting me to kiss her. It was such a clear invitation.

It would be an insult not to accept such a sweet invitation.

I closed the distance between us and pressed my lips softly against hers.

She smiled. I felt her lips smile against mine.

"You're smiling," I said.

"I'm happy."

In that case, I kissed her again.

There was a hurricane bearing down on us. She'd been left at the altar yesterday. And there was a ghost in her house who seemed to have an uncanny sense of predicting an impending storm.

And yet through all that, I'd kissed her and she was happy.

And that made me happy.

Happier than I had been in a really long time.

My phone rang.

"I need to…" I pulled away and took my phone from my front pocket. "It's my friend."

"Of course," she said.

She turned and walked away from me, giving me privacy. I didn't need it, but she gave it to me.

"Hey Daniel," I said, putting a hand over my other ear to keep the roar of the wind out. "Did you find out anything?"

"Yes," Daniel said. "But you aren't going to like it."

20

ISLA

I couldn't hear their words, but I could tell by the tone and by the expression on Christopher's face that the news wasn't good.

His friend was in the national guard and the national guard was being deployed to Louisiana. So bad news on that front was to be expected.

I stood facing the wind, letting the soft breeze that smelled of salt and a faint hint of fish wash over me.

Clouds were moving this way. Bands of white clouds. The outer bands.

They said the storm was slowing, but whoever they were didn't seem to quite know which way was up.

Right now, though, at this particular moment, none of that frightened me.

As I'd told Christopher, I was happy.

I'd pretty much forgotten what happiness felt like.

I could still feel his lips on mine. Tender. Soft.

Not what I would have expected from being kissed by a military man, veteran or not. Not that I would know, since he was the first soldier of any kind that I had ever kissed.

I kind of liked the idea.

My grandpa had been a soldier and he was one of the best men I had ever known.

They didn't make them like that anymore.

The wind carried an energy. Either that or my blood was on fire from kissing Christopher. Maybe a little bit of both.

It was a heady mixture.

After ending his phone call, he came up and stood next to me.

"It looks so calm, doesn't it?" he asked.

"Deceptively so," I said. "Your friend can't help us?"

"No."

I looked up at him sideways.

"He's on his way to Louisiana, isn't he?"

"You're very perceptive," he said.

"And yet the storm is coming toward us."

"Again," he said, sweeping a strand of hair off my face. "Pretty and smart."

"You're trying to distract me."

"Is it working?"

"Maybe a little," I said. Actually a lot. "What's your plan B?"

"What makes you think I have a plan B?"

A flock of seagulls passed overhead, making a lot of racket and a car passed in the distance. Normal sounds. But that normal was temporary.

"Because you're too calm."

"Maybe you make me calm."

"So when you're being quiet, you're sharpening your witty tongue."

"I do not have a witty tongue."

"How about charming?" I asked, smiling up at him.

"I'll take charming," he said. "Especially since I'm about to rescue a damsel in distress."

"I'm not—"

He put a finger over my lips.

"Don't go all politically correct on me," he said. "A man needs to feel needed once in a while."

"I strongly suspect you get to feel needed a great deal."

"Maybe," he said. "But not by a girl as beautiful as you."

21

CHRISTOPHER

Having officially evacuated and locked up my rental cottage, I stashed my gear beneath the Denton's coffee table and made myself at home on their couch.

After lunch, the whole family, Isla included, went upstairs to take a nap. Very unusual. But endearing at the same time.

My mother didn't believe in naps, so we didn't get to sleep during the day.

I pulled out my iPad and did some research. I wanted to exhaust all my options before I called Grandpa Noah. And I wasn't even going to think about calling my father. Quinn Worthington was not what one would call a forgiving father. He was a good father as long as we all did what we were supposed to do.

But it was my grandfather that I would call in a pinch and this was definitely a pinch.

Growing up around pilots and then being an officer in the Air Force, I'd become something of a weather aficionado. I'd learned to read the radar, wind speed, temperature, and bring it all together. I pulled out a pad of paper and pen and with my iPad open, got to work.

The branches of the palm trees were hitting the windows now and the wind was howling around the corner of the house. A storm was most definitely on the way.

Fortunately, I didn't hear any sounds coming from Ophelia. That could be because Isla was sleeping in the room above where Ophelia spent her time in eternity packing.

It seemed like such a horrible way to spend eternity. I hoped if had the opportunity to haunt a place, I'd have less work to do.

It didn't seem to bother Isla to sleep in the room where a ghost supposedly lived. She'd grown up with the stories. And the sounds.

It actually frightened me a bit that Ophelia was quiet while Isla slept. It provided evidence, to my way of thinking, that Ophelia's ghost—a considerate ghost—really did exist.

I took a long drink of water and found my thoughts back on Isla.

Now that I'd kissed her, my head was even more full of her. I replayed that kiss over and over. I'd had to kiss her. It would have been ungentlemanly not to.

I smiled to myself at the oddity of that way of thinking.

But she'd turned her face up to mine and she was so beautiful.

I would never tire of kissing her. Of just looking at her.

It was funny, because I didn't even know what kind of work she did. And I didn't care.

She could be a server at a diner or a brain surgeon or anything in between. She was still the most adorable woman I had ever met.

She would just have to get used to having me around. And after she did, I'd talk her into marrying me.

Now that I had that figured out, I settled back down and got to work on making my own weather forecast.

An hour later, I sat back and stared at the screen.

Surely not.

I double-checked my work. But I had it right.

We were in more danger than anyone was predicting.

ISLA

ost people would probably protest sleeping in the bedroom where a ghost was known to frequent. Especially when the ghost was in an active state.

But Ophelia didn't frighten me.

I'd never told a soul, but I had seen her once. When I was a child. Eight years old.

I knew now that ghosts were most likely to show themselves to children, so I figured that's what had happened.

I'd woke in the middle of the night. I remembered it well. There had been a full moon, shining bright through my window and I had thought that was what had woken me.

But when I turned over and looked toward the open door, I'd seen her.

Ophelia was standing in the doorway watching me. She was stunningly beautiful and she literally glowed. I'd known immediately that she wasn't a person.

I'd heard the story and knew that a ghost was rumored to live in the house.

She'd been somewhat transparent. Almost like what I

imagined a holograph might look like. She smiled at me and held out her hand.

That part had startled me. I remember thinking that she'd come to take me with her. But, of course, that hadn't been it.

She'd been holding out a letter.

I didn't move. I just lay there, frozen. Not knowing what to do.

Then she was gone.

The carefully folded letter fluttered to the floor.

I'd lain there in my bed for a long time staring at the letter on the floor. Waiting for it disappear or for her to come back for it.

When neither happened, I'd fallen asleep.

When I woke the next morning and remembered it as I got my bearings, I'd thought it was a dream. But the letter was still there.

I still had it. And I had it memorized.

Dear Charles,

They tell us there is a storm coming. A very bad storm. They want us to leave. I don't want to leave the home we built together, but I will. I'll leave it if it means we can be together again.

So I'm putting everything important in boxes to take with me to my sister's house in Houston. I can't stand the thought of having everything destroyed by water damage.

Also, there's something very important I need to tell you, but I'll wait until we're together again.

I love you more than life itself.

Ophelia

·   ·   ·

My childhood imagination had filled in the blanks over the years. I'd imagined all sorts of things that could be important for her to want to tell him.

Maybe they were having a baby. That was my favorite one. And the one I kept coming back to over and over.

It broke my heart that she never got to tell him and that they never got to be together again.

It was a travesty that she somehow had to spend eternity packing up a house. What a horrible thing to have to do.

I wished her peace and told her so quite often in the darkness of night when I was here alone. I'd even looked up Charles Bridges, but he'd never made it home. He'd been killed in the war. I don't think he ever even got her letter.

How could he have gotten it when I had it?

I'd always wondered what a love like that would feel like.

And now I knew. It was all-encompassing. It was everything.

I knew because that's how I felt when I was with Christopher.

Like he was everything.

23

———

CHRISTOPHER

I'd just hung up the phone from talking with my grandfather when Aunt Mae came downstairs from her nap.

"No coffee," she murmured as she proceeded to get the can from the cabinet and make coffee herself.

"Sorry," I said. "If I'd known, I would have made it."

"I'm not blaming you," she said, turning and leaning against the cabinet while she studied me.

I sat at the kitchen table, one hand over my phone.

"You look troubled," she said.

"For good reason," I said with a glance out the window behind her.

"Any updates?" she asked.

"They're still saying the same."

"You don't believe them," she said, squinting at me.

"You take after your niece," I said with a little laugh.

"Speaking of," she said, grabbing a quick cup of just brewed coffee and sitting down next to me. "Do you mind if I ask you a personal question?"

"Would you ask anyway?"

"No." Aunt Mae smiled and took a sip of the steaming coffee.

I leaned back. Waited for whatever it was she wanted to ask me.

"Are you the reason Franklin didn't show up to the wedding?"

I hadn't been expecting that question. It hadn't even occurred to me that someone would think that.

"No," I said.

She smiled and looked over her cup at me.

"How long have you known Isla?"

"Not long," I said, hedging.

She narrowed her eyes at me again. "More than a day?"

I shook my head, deciding it didn't matter if they knew I'd just met her.

"So you just followed the girl home?"

I shrugged. "She seemed like she needed the company."

"And now you're still here." There was no animosity in her tone. Just curiosity.

"You have to admit, she's an intriguing, beautiful woman."

"Never denied that," she said. "But she doesn't need to be hurt a second time. Not right on the heels of that cad Franklin."

"Agreed," I said. "You didn't like Franklin?"

"Never trusted the guy and it seemed my intuition was right."

"So it seems," I said.

"Don't hurt my girl," she said.

"I don't plan on hurting her. You don't have to worry about that."

"You haven't known her long enough to have intentions," she said. "So I won't ask you that."

I nodded once, in appreciation.

Then we both turned to see Isla standing in the door, looking at us curiously.

24

ISLA

It was little disconcerting seeing my aunt talking to Christopher. Aunt Mae took no prisoners. She said what she had to say without hesitation.

"Want some coffee?" Aunt Mae asked me.

"Sure," I said. I didn't normally drink coffee in the afternoons, but it was probably going to be a long day and I was still feeling a little fuzzy from my nap.

As she got up and poured coffee into a mug and some milk in the frother, I sat down next to Christopher.

"Hi," I said.

"Hi." He smiled at me, then looked away as Aunt Mae set the coffee cup in front of me.

I narrowed my eyes at Aunt Mae. She just shrugged.

"I'm going upstairs to start packing," she said, taking her coffee with her.

"Did she give you a hard time?" I asked, carefully sipping the steaming hot coffee.

"Nothing I couldn't handle," he said.

"Good." I sat back. Looked at him. "You look troubled."

"You're the second person to tell me that in the last half hour."

"Then it must true." I said with a little smile.

"It is true," he said.

"But you'd rather we didn't notice."

A box fell onto the floor overhead.

"I'm guessing that's not your aunt doing that," he said.

"You'd be guessing right."

"So…" I said. "I have something I thought you might want to see."

"What is it?"

"First," I said. "You have to know that I've had this since I was eight-years-old and I've never shown anyone."

"Not even Franklin?" he asked.

"No. Not even Franklin." I studied my coffee, deciding it was a fair enough question. "He wouldn't have appreciated it."

"What is it?" he asked again.

I reached into my back pocket and pulled out the letter I'd kept since I was a child. Since that night I'd seen Ophelia standing in my bedroom doorway. It had been new when I'd first picked it up off the floor, but now it was faded from the years and worn from the dozens of times I'd unfolded it and read it.

I opened it. smoothed it out and laid in front of him.

He read it through then looked up at me.

"Where did you get this?"

"She gave it to me."

A box slid across the floor. Another one landed with a thump.

"What do you think the secret was?"

I shook my head. "I guess we'll never know."

"It's heartbreaking," he said, reading the letter again.

After he finished, he looked up at me. "You think they were going to have a baby."

"It's the most logical thing, don't you think?"

"It might explain why she's so determined to wait for him."

"Good point."

"I wish there was some way we could help her," he said. "I hate the thought of her spending eternity moving boxes."

"Me too."

"So when she gave you letter," he said. "did you see her?"

25

CHRISTOPHER

Shivers ran down my spine as Isla told me the story of how Ophelia had come to her door and dropped the letter there.

"Did you ever see her again?" I asked. The thought of seeing a ghost frightened the hell out of me and I was man enough to admit it, at least to myself.

I'd never been afraid facing the enemy in battle, but facing something I didn't understand was something else entirely.

"No," she said. "that was the one and only time."

"Does it scare you?" I asked. "Knowing that she's here?"

The letter was handwritten in an old ink-smeared script. Faded and worn from being unfolded and refolded over the years.

"She doesn't scare me," she said. "I was terrified that night. But after I read the letter, I understood why she was still here and I wasn't afraid anymore."

I nodded. "You're very brave."

"I'm not so brave."

"From where I'm sitting, it looks like you are."

"I'm just an ordinary girl doing ordinary things."

I doubted that was true. She seemed anything other than ordinary to me.

"What kind of work do you do?" I asked.

"I have a job in marketing with a big firm in Houston."

"You like it?"

"I like it. I work with some good people and the work allows me to be creative."

"I feel like I'm starting over now that I'm *retired.*"

She smiled a little. "It must be strange to be retired at such a young age."

"It is."

"What are you going to do?" she asked.

"That's what I'm here to figure out," I said. "At least it was what I was here to figure out."

"Now we have other things to worry about."

I looked over her shoulder and lowered my voice. "Do you want to see my forecast?"

"Sure."

Leading her out to the living room, I was still wavering on whether or not I wanted to tell her what I had found out about the hurricane.

First, I didn't want to frighten her any more than she already was and second, I wasn't a meteorologist, so my forecast held no merit other than my own rudimentary calculations.

But she'd shown me her letter from Ophelia.

After sitting on the couch, side by side, I opened my iPad.

"You've been busy," she said, looking at my handwritten notes and formulas on the paper.

"Yeah. It's kind of a hobby."

"Looks like more than a hobby."

"I think the weather forecasters either have it wrong or they aren't telling us everything."

"What is it?" she asked, squinting at the program on my iPad.

A box fell overhead and we both looked up. Ophelia was making her presence known.

I wondered if there was anything anyone could do to help her.

"Do you have a picture of her? Of Ophelia?"

"I think so. Somewhere."

"Can I see it?" I asked. "Later?"

She nodded and I proceeded to show her what I'd calculated in terms of the storm.

26

ISLA

"Are you sure?" she asked, peering at my iPad screen."

"No," I said. "I'm not sure of anything."

"Well… maybe you should tell someone."

"Maybe. But they'll figure it out if they haven't already."

They had to know. From what Christopher was showing me, it was quite clear.

There were two distinct eyes. Two hurricanes.

It was like a zygote that had transformed into two identical twins.

"Has this ever happened before?" I asked.

"I don't think so. I did some research. Hurricanes have merged before, but I couldn't find any evidence of one splitting like this."

"If you're right," I asked. "And no offense, but I hope you aren't, what does that mean?"

"I means there could be a landfall in Louisiana like they're saying, but there could also be a landfall here."

"We need to get out of here," I said. My words were punctuated by boxes sliding overhead. Ophelia, it seemed, agreed with me.

"Can you be ready in…" he glanced at his watch. "three hours?"

"I'm ready now."

He smiled. "Good. Can your family be ready?"

"I'm sure." I stood up and he stood up with me. "How much can they take?"

"Just a bag each," he said.

I started to go. To tell my parents and my aunt that we were leaving. But I needed to know more. I needed to know how.

"How?" I asked.

"There's a boat on the way."

"A boat," I said, immediately picturing a little fishing boat. My skepticism must have shown in my expression.

"Either a boat or a helicopter. The details aren't quite finalized."

"Don't worry," he said. "It will be a big enough boat… or helicopter for everyone."

I nodded. Then walked over to stand in front of him.

"Thank you," I said.

"You don't have to tha—"

I put a hand on his cheek to pull him down for a kiss.

Then I smiled into his eyes.

"What were you going to say?"

"Nothing," he said. "Not a thing."

I grinned. "I'll go make sure everyone gets their things packed up."

"Good. If there are keepsakes you want to bring. A box or something. I'm sure we can find room."

Ophelia dropped a box overhead and we both smiled at each other.

"This weekend has turned out to be a whole lot more interesting than I thought it was going to be."

"All things considering," he said. "That's saying quite a bit."

It was saying quite a bit indeed, I thought as I made my way back upstairs.

I'd gone from almost getting married to crushing on a complete stranger.

Sometimes life was funny that way.

Things didn't turn out the way we expected them to.

And everything happened for a reason.

I had to believe that.

Otherwise, there were far too many coincidences.

27

CHRISTOPHER

*J*ust two hours later, Mr. Denton and I had dragged a half a dozen suitcases out to the beach as well as one large plastic tote.

The Dentons had a few things they wanted to save… just in case… and I assured them that the boat or the helicopter could handle it.

The wind was picking up a bit now and the beach was deserted. People were busy boarding up their windows and preparing to hunker down. The sound of hammers echoed along the beach.

They really had no choice at this point except to prepare to ride out the storm.

But I'd given us a choice.

I'd called Grandpa Noah and he had immediately set things in motion. Either a boat or a helicopter would be here to pick us up in little more than an hour. Grandpa had been specific on the time, but he had two options on the mode of transportation.

Mr. and Mrs. Denton sat together on a blanket, their heads bent together in quiet conversation. Aunt Mae paced back and forth to the house, her cell phone pressed against her ear, talking to somebody.

Isla and I walked down the beach.

"Are you okay?" I asked.

She leaned close, bumped my arm with her shoulder.

"It's a beautiful day," she said, looking up at the bright sun overhead.

It was almost unimaginable that there was a deadly storm just hours away.

I took her hand in mine, decided it felt right. If I put the storm in the back of my mind, I could imagine that we were just a normal couple walking along a normal beach on a normal day.

We turned around and started back the way we had come.

The sound of a power saw blended with the soothing sound of the waves crashing ashore, a reminder of the destruction brewing out at sea.

I caught sight of a boat coming this way, following the shoreline, several yards out. It was too far away for me to tell what kind of boat it was, but it was definitely moving steadily in this direction. This would be our ride.

That meant my time on the island was drawing to a close as was my time with Isla. She'd go back to her life and I'd be spending time catching up with my family, long overdue as it was.

I wasn't quite ready to let this moment go.

"How long do you think Ophelia will be stuck here, packing boxes and preparing to leave the island?"

"I don't know," she said. "She's been here well over a century. She might always be here."

"Do you know when the house was built?"

"Late 1800s," she said. "It would have been a fairly new house when the storm hit. I think she and her husband built it together."

She stopped and reached into the handbag draped across her shoulders. "I found this."

She held out a black and white photograph of a young lady, fashionably dressed for her time period.

I took the photograph and studied it.

"I can see the resemblance," I said. "She's beautiful like you."

Isla grinned and took the photograph back.

"You're being charming again."

"Am I?"

She smiled.

I watched the boat out of the corner of my eyes.

It was getting closer now. Close enough that I could see that it was a yacht. My grandfather would send no less.

"After we get back to Houston, do—"

"Look," she said, pointing to the boat I'd been watching. "There's a boat." She looked at me. "Is that our boat?"

"Most likely," I said.

Whatever I was about to ask would have to wait.

28

ISLA

Seagulls circled overhead, squawking and making all sorts of noise. Behind us, the air was filled with hammering and sawing as people prepared to board up their homes to ride out the storm.

The waves were coming in harder now, crashing against the shore. Sure signs of the storm to come.

The boat that had come for us was not an ordinary boat. It was a yacht. In all my years visiting the ocean with my parents, I'd never been on a yacht.

Jet skis. A sailboat. But no yacht.

Christopher and I stood with my parents and Aunt Mae as they anchored the yacht and lowered a small boat, a dinghy, to the water.

"Do you know the captain?" I asked.

"I don't know. Maybe."

He glanced at his phone. "They're a little early."

"It's okay," I said. "Right?"

I was feeling a little nervous about meeting someone Christopher knew. Maybe even someone in his family.

Either way, I couldn't deny the nerves I was feeling.

Christopher looked decidedly troubled.

I would have time to talk to him on the ride to Galveston.

Two people were coming ashore in the dinghy.

A tingle of apprehension skittered up my spine.

Something seemed… off.

As the dinghy got closer, I put a hand over my eyes and my heart sank.

This was not supposed to be.

"It can't be," I said to myself.

"What can't be?" Christopher asked automatically, but he was looking troubled, too.

When the boat reached the beach and one of the men tossed out an anchor, none of us moved.

"It's Franklin," I said.

Christopher looked down at me. "Your Franklin?"

"Yes," I said, feeling decidedly angry and disappointed and just generally, well… angry.

Franklin jumped out of the boat and came straight toward me.

Even though I felt like recoiling, I stood my ground and kept my chin up.

"What are you doing here?" I asked.

"I was in an accident," he said, pointing to the bruise on his cheek. "And I lost my phone."

I just stared at him.

"I didn't have your phone number."

Franklin looked from me to Christopher.

"I'm sorry," he said. "But I'm here now. And there is a hurricane headed this way."

"Well," Aunt Mae said. "It's about time."

Another dinghy pulled up beside the first one and before I knew what was happening, the two men were gathering up our luggage and had it loaded onto the second boat.

"Come on," Daddy said. "Let's get out of here."

29

CHRISTOPHER

The yacht was quickly becoming no more than a distant speck on the horizon. Traveling close to the shoreline, the yacht passed the carnival, sitting still and quiet, and kept going.

Seagulls squawked overhead, soaring and playing in the strong wind. That wouldn't last long. They would be moving inland before long along with anyone and anything that could.

Water splashed over my sneakers as I stood still, watching the yacht that carried Isla away from me.

I was feeling sick. A tug on my heartstrings as she moved further and further away.

Her fiancé had left her at the altar, but he had a good reason. He'd been in an accident and had not been able to get in touch with her.

Not likely, but possible. If I lost my cell phone, I, too, would be at a loss, since I didn't have anyone's phone numbers memorized. Fortunately, I could always call Skye Travels and get the phone number for anyone in my family. I had a significant advantage in that way.

But... what I couldn't figure out was why. My head was still reeling. I'd gotten the sense from Isla that she was anything but heartbroken about Franklin not showing up for the wedding.

She had told me she was happy.

And she had invited me to kiss her.

No. I was certain she was not heartbroken.

Yet she had gone with him.

Maybe she hadn't known what else to do with her family standing there, pulling her along with them.

And I played my own part in the whole thing.

She'd looked at me, her emerald green eyes searching mine, but I hadn't reacted. I'd shown no reaction at all.

If she had been looking for me to say something... anything... that might lead her believe that I didn't want her to go, then she was disappointed.

I'd just stood there, frozen, not knowing what to do or say.

I realized now that I had been stunned into paralysis.

Franklin was her fiancé, for God's sake. What was I supposed to do? I wasn't going to come between the two of them.

I'd wanted to. I'd wanted to tell her not to go. To stay with me. but before I could form the words, making the words out of whole cloth feelings, she was gone.

I walked back toward the Denton's house and sat down on the front steps to wait for my own ride out of here.

Although the house was locked up, I heard a stack of boxes falling onto the second-story floor.

I smiled to myself. Ophelia wanted out of here, too. If I could take her with me, I would. Set her up someplace where she could enjoy eternity without so much work.

Morbid as it was, I found myself wondering exactly how she had died. The house had withstood the hurricane, but she hadn't. What had happened?

As I sat there contemplating two women. Ophelia and Isla, I heard the whirring of helicopter blades coming this way.

As the helicopter landed in front of the house, sand went everywhere. I pulled out my shades and put them over my eyes.

I didn't know the pilot. Skye Travels didn't do helicopters. Fortunately, my grandfather knew everybody and helping out Noah Worthington was seen by many as an honor.

As the helicopter left the ground with me safely inside, sweeping toward past the house, I looked down.

And I swear upon everything that was holy, I saw Ophelia standing at the second-floor window, one hand holding the curtains back, looking right at me.

30

ISLA

I sat in silence, staring back at the beach until I couldn't see Christopher anymore.

My heart ached as we got further and further away.

It was insanity. The man I had planned to marry just two days ago had come to my rescue. Yet, I felt nothing for him.

My heart yearned for the troubled veteran standing on the beach.

If he had given me so much as an inkling that he wanted me to stay. To not leave with Franklin. I would have stayed.

I would have let my family go with Franklin if they wanted to. Or they would have been welcome to wait and go with Christopher. He had assured me that he had secured transportation for all of us.

But he hadn't. Daddy had urged me along and without any sign whatsoever from Christopher, I had gone with Franklin.

It all happened so fast.

As we approached the main island of Galveston, I turned around and studied Franklin. He was wearing khaki shorts and a white button-down shirt. Shades over his eyes, his perfectly cut hair that he got trimmed and styled every

Friday. A confident expression on his face as he navigated the boat.

I hadn't even known Franklin knew how to drive a yacht.

But he was doing it and he looked overconfident. Self-assured.

He winked at me when he saw me watching him. The bruise on the side of his forehead did nothing to take away from his handsomeness.

And yet, I felt nothing for him.

I had felt everything for Christopher.

After the boat was secure and we made our way to the two SUVs that would take us away from the ocean, I felt empty.

Traffic was backed up with people evacuating Galveston and cars were moving at a snail's pace. They were in the process of opening the southbound lane of the freeway, but that hadn't happened yet.

They were going to have to do it soon or we would never get out of here.

As I sat there next to Franklin, I stared out the window thinking about Christopher.

It hit me like a load of bricks that not only did I not have Christopher's phone number, nor did he have mine, but I didn't even know his last name.

He knew mine, but he would have no idea how to find me in Houston, a city with millions of people. The only thing he knew about me was that I worked for a marketing company.

There were hundreds of marketing companies in the city of Houston.

Franklin sat next to me in the back seat of one of the late model SUVs that still had that new car scent. Franklin came from a family of new wealth. His father had fallen into some money and Franklin had ridden on his coattails.

As we traveled away from the ocean, away from Christopher, I wondered what I had seen in Franklin. I'd gotten comfortable. That was it. I'd gotten comfortable and things had just moved along of their own accord.

"I'll make it up to you," Franklin said.

I tried to smile. But I was pretty sure my feeble attempt came out upside down.

I had to reconcile myself to never seeing Christopher again.

And that shattered my heart.

31

CHRISTOPHER

The city of Houston was shut down while the outer bands of the hurricane brought rain and wind. There was no evacuation order for Houston, just the recommendation that everyone stay home and stay off the roads. Stay inside. So far there had been no reports of power outages.

Galveston, on the other hand, had a mandatory evacuation order that had come in shortly after Isla and I had gotten off the island. And according to the images on the Weather Channel it was mayhem down there.

The hotels and shelters in Houston were overflowing. People out of Galveston heading north and west to try to find a place, anyplace to stay other than in their vehicles.

I wondered what the people on the other side of West Beach Bridge had done. I hoped that the national guard had gotten them out of there. If the stretch of island had had anything resembling an airport, we could have gotten them out. Unfortunately, that wasn't an option.

I sat at the kitchen table with Grandma Savannah and Grandpa Noah.

The kitchen that usually smelled like fresh baked apple pie, smelled like coffee, toast, and bacon.

I was freshly showered and dressed for the day. I should have felt better. I should have felt relieved.

But my heart was heavy.

"Have you thought about what you're going to do now?" Grandma Savannah asked as she slid into the chair next to mine.

I had expected the question. Something would have been wrong if I hadn't gotten it.

And Grandpa Savannah, nearly seventy years old, was still beautiful and she asked so nicely with a lovely smile, I couldn't not at least try to answer.

"I honestly have no idea," I said, looking into those deep green eyes that could see deep into a person's psyche. She used that natural talent to supplement her training as a psychologist. It would be a loss to humanity if she ever decided to retire, which she wouldn't.

She put a slice of bacon on my plate and one on hers.

I looked at Grandpa sitting with a piece of toast on his plate.

"He can't have bacon," she said with a little nonchalant shrug. "Doctor's orders."

"Ouch," I said. "Bacon is one of life's little pleasures."

Grandpa shot us a look as he got up and went to the refrigerator.

"You don't have to rush," Grandma Savannah said. "You'll figure out what you want to do in due time."

"I know," I said. "Thank you for saying so."

Grandpa came back and sat down with a glass of bubbling orange juice.

"What is that?" Grandma Savannah asked him.

"A mimosa," he said, taking a sip. "Wasn't on the list of restricted items."

"Incorrigible," she said. "Always has been. Always will be."

"You wouldn't have him any other way."

"You're so right," she said, leaning back and taking a bite of her bacon.

Grandma and Grandpa had an interesting story. They'd been college sweethearts separated by some kind of family thing. Lost touch.

Then, with all odds against them, they'd spotted each other in a crowded airport. The rest was history. Five children. Loads of grandchildren. Great grandchildren coming on a regular basis.

All was good in their world.

They were living their happily-ever-after.

I had a very distinct feeling that I had let my happily-ever-after get on a yacht in Galveston and disappear out of my life.

All I knew was her name.

Isla Denton.

Enchanting barefoot bride who wasn't a bride.

32

ISLA

It was probably a little cold-hearted, but I'd let Franklin drive me to my apartment.

After he'd parked and helped me get my suitcase inside, I turned and leaned against my armchair, looking at him.

"Want to get some dinner?" he asked.

"No. I have some things to do."

"What?" he asked.

"Things." A wedding to unravel.

"Okay." He lightly touched the bruise on his cheek. "Maybe later."

I walked to the door. Put my hand on the doorknob. "Thanks for the ride," I said.

"You're mad," he said.

I should be mad, but I wasn't. I just didn't want to be around Franklin right now. Maybe never.

Something had shifted for me while I'd walked barefoot on the beach in my wedding dress. Alone.

It had shifted even further when I'd kissed Christopher. That's when everything had changed permanently.

If not for Christopher, I might would have been

understanding of Franklin's plight and I might would have forgiven him.

I was, after all, quite forgiving. I'd forgiven Franklin his workaholism. I'd reframed it into calling it his drive.

"I'm not mad," I said. "I just woke up."

He had the decency to look stunned. "What does that mean?"

"It means we need to take a break," I said. "Reassess."

"Reassess," he repeated.

I opened the door.

"I'm tired, Franklin. I'm just going to take a long hot bath and go to bed."

"I could—"

I held up a finger. "Alone."

He wasn't happy about it, but he left anyway.

I stood with my back to the locked door until I heard him drive away.

Then I decided that taking a hot bath really was a good idea.

But I didn't go to bed afterwards.

Instead, I got on my computer and searched for a man named Christopher who lived in Houston.

A needle in a haystack.

I'd known it was futile when I started, but I'd had to try.

Once in a while, when it was meant to be, a girl got lucky.

But not this time.

So instead, I did some reading on the 1900 hurricane that had wiped out most of Galveston.

On all accounts, I'd been right. They hadn't even seen it coming.

Sick to my stomach, I closed the lid on my computer and went in search of something to eat.

Since I'd planned on being on my honeymoon right about now, there was nothing in my refrigerator.

With the hurricane on the way, the stores were going to be

packed. And the delivery services were already overwhelmed to the point of being useless.

I grabbed my keys and left my apartment, deciding I had no choice but to brave the grocery store before everything closed down.

33

CHRISTOPHER

The next morning after the worst of the hurricane had passed through, I went outside with Grandpa to assess the damage.

The courtyard surrounded by the house on all four sides, was soaked, but otherwise untouched. There was, however, a tree down in the back yard.

"Guess we slept through all this," I said, picking up a limb and tossing it onto the tree."

"Glad somebody slept," he said.

"You didn't?" I asked, turning to look at him. It had been a handful of years since I'd seen him and I could see those years on him. He still looked good for a man approaching seventy years old. Grandpa Noah was one of a kind.

"Sat up most of the night," he said. "Watched over your grandmother while she slept."

It didn't surprise me. Not really.

The love my grandparents shared for each other was well known to the point of being legendary.

"If I'd known, I would have stayed up with you," I said. I was supposed to be the soldier after all.

"It's okay," he said. "I knew where to find you if anything happened."

"Hmm." For some reason, Isla had come to my mind.

I would stay up all night to make sure she was safe.

I'd screwed up. I'd let her go and I didn't know where to find her.

She was somewhere in the city. That was all I knew. But I did know her name. I hadn't googled her yet, but I would.

And if… when… I found her, I didn't know what I would do. But I had a feeling I wasn't going to just let her go that easily.

I told myself I needed to give her time to sort out what she was going to do about Franklin.

I didn't think I should muddy the water there.

But being here and being reminded of the love my grandparents had for each other was just about all the motivation I needed to give myself permission to seek Isla out.

And who knows, maybe muddying the water wasn't such a bad thing to do.

"It's good having you back," Grandpa Noah said, clapping me on the back.

"It's good to be back."

"Maybe you'll stay around this time."

"Maybe I will."

"Just let me know what you decide to do. I'll be behind you one hundred percent."

"I know. Thank you."

I might be retired at thirty-three, but Worthingtons didn't retire.

"Let's go back inside," he said. "I need to call somebody to come clean this mess up. Then you can tell me what happened in Galveston."

I nearly missed a step.

"What do you mean?" I asked.

"I've known you a long time, Grandson," he said with a little smile on his lips. "And I know that look."

I fell into step beside him, wondering at Noah Worthington's uncanny sense about people. In some ways, it was stronger than Grandma Savannah's and she was a psychologist.

"Besides," he said as we passed the swimming pool filled with debris from the storm. "You said you needed transportation for five."

34

ISLA

I sat at my office desk overlooking the 610 freeway and tapped my pen against the pad of legal paper. I was supposed to be preparing a presentation, but my mind wasn't on it. In my defense, I was actually supposed to be on my honeymoon right now.

I'd gotten some funny looks when I came into work this morning, but it was easy enough to blame it on the hurricane. All flights had been canceled, so no one seemed surprised and no one said anything about my bare ring finger.

Everybody seemed to be lost in their own thoughts. A lot of people were still off work, dealing with post storm clean up.

The freeway was back to normal. Busy. Flashing lights next to a fender bender. Back to normal.

But I wasn't back to normal.

My normal was so off-kilter, I couldn't even see it anymore.

Oddly enough, I hadn't even heard from Franklin. I found that disconcerting. I thought he would have at least fought for me. A little bit.

It was easier this way, I told myself. He'd saved me the difficult task of telling him I not only didn't want to marry him, I didn't want to date him anymore. It seemed he had gotten the idea.

Since I wasn't getting any work done, I decided to go get something for lunch.

"Do you want me to bring you something back?" I asked Trudy, the receptionist.

"Sure," she said. "Going next door?"

"Yeah, just need a break."

"The usual if you don't mind."

"I don't."

"It's my turn to buy," she said, pulling out a twenty and sliding it across the counter.

"Are you sure?" I asked. "I need to start keeping track better."

"Don't worry," she said. "All you need is one more thing on your mind. Oh." She held up a finger as she answered the phone.

I waited as she deftly answered the phone and transferred the call to the right department.

Trudy kept the reception area clean. One day, I swore, I'd ask her to help me organize my office.

"Someone called and asked about you."

"A client?"

"I don't think so," she said, staring thoughtfully into space. "He asked personal questions about you."

A little shiver of alarm ran up my spine. "What kind of personal questions?"

"Well. First he asked if you were working today and I said yes, not thinking anything about it. Then he asked if you'd gotten married over the weekend."

"What did you tell him?"

"I told him that was personal and he'd have to ask you himself if he wanted to know something that personal about you."

"Probably just a client," I said. "I'm sure some of them knew I was supposed to get married."

"Yeah," Trudy said. "No. I don't think so."

"Why not?"

"I asked if he wanted to make an appointment."

"Did he?"

"Oddly enough, no. I asked if he needed anything else. He said no, thanked me, and hung up. He was very nice."

"That is a little strange," I said, but I shrugged it off. Could have been anything. "Thanks for telling me."

35

CHRISTOPHER

It took only a couple of days for Houston to get itself back to some semblance of normality. Galveston, according to the news, was a different story. Still struggling. But thankfully no reports of casualties. Someone must have gotten the people off the island. Either that or they had hunkered down and managed to survive.

I stayed with my grandparents and dealt with the rental car I'd left on the island. Apparently they had insurance for this kind of thing, but there was paperwork involved. Seemed like nothing could be easy.

But the sun was shining and I had time to catch up with family without the pressure of knowing I had to leave. A luxury I barely knew what to do with.

It hadn't taken me long to find Isla. It was actually a little bit frightening how easy it had been to find her. But her name was unusual and she worked in the public arena.

The hard part was trying to figure out what to do about her.

I still had a sense of honor, misplaced or not, that I should give her time.

Then I'd remember the way her lips felt on mine and that resolve would vanish.

So I was torn.

Eventually my sense of honor bowed to my need to see her again.

She worked in an office just ten, maybe fifteen minutes from my grandparents' house.

It was amazing to me that I had been all over the world and the woman I had fallen in love with had been right here in Houston all along.

It might be premature to call it love, but I didn't know what else to call it.

I thought about her all the time. I dreamed about her at night. I daydreamed about a future with her. Watching my grandparents made those daydreams all that much stronger.

I knew what a good relationship looked like. I knew what it took.

And I was ready to get on with it.

I'd sowed my oats. And I knew what I wanted.

All I had to do was to figure out how to make it happen.

It was a cool evening, a few days after the storm. I sat with Grandpa Noah in the courtyard in front of a fire in a pit.

He'd sent me inside for a couple of beers.

"Are you supposed to have that?" I asked as I handed him the bottle.

"Probably not," he said. "Just don't tell your grandmother and everything will be just fine."

I laughed. "I won't tell her."

If not telling Grandma he had a beer was the worst thing he kept from her, then he was an admirable man indeed.

I stretched out my legs and listened to the crickets that had somehow gotten into Grandma's flowers.

"How do crickets get in here?" I asked. The courtyard, the

middle of the house, had no direct access to the outside other than an open roof.

"Hell if I know," he said. "Lightning bugs, too."

"I get those," I said. "They can fly. But I don't get the crickets."

"I think they can fly," Grandpa Noah said.

I considered that. "Maybe they climb over the walls."

"Maybe." He stretched out and savored his beer. "Have you found that girl yet?"

"I did."

"And?"

"Not sure what that *and* is yet."

"Not like you to be indecisive," he said.

"It's not that I'm indecisive," I said. "It's just that I don't know what the next step is."

He grinned at me and I just shrugged.

"What would you do?" I asked.

"That's easy," he said. "I'd go get her."

ISLA

The next morning I sat at my desk, staring out the window again. I wasn't going to get much work done at this rate.

I had a phone number. Trudy had looked back at the caller ID and given me the phone number of the man who had called asking about me.

Scribbled on a post-it note, it sat right there in the middle of my desk.

I'd had it now for going on twenty-four hours and I hadn't called it.

I wanted to know, but if it wasn't Christopher, I didn't want to know. As long as I didn't know, the number held possibilities.

"Enough is enough," I said, picking up my cell phone and entering the number.

Taking a deep breath, I dialed the number.

"Skye Travels."

I held the phone away from my ear and glared at it. Skye Travels?

"I'm sorry," I said. "I have the wrong number." I hung up the phone and closed my eyes.

So maybe he'd called me on his way out to… anywhere. Skye Travels was the premier private aviation company in Houston and maybe even in the country.

If the phone call had been made by Christopher and he had been on his way somewhere else, there were so many implications about that.

First of all, that meant he wasn't here in Houston. He might even live somewhere else. Had he told me he lived in Houston? I couldn't remember. There had been a lot going on and my memory was fuzzy about some of the details.

And second of all, if he'd flown with Skye Travels, that meant he could afford to fly private.

All in all, this added up to one conclusion.

I wasn't going to see him again.

Even if he did live here in Houston, if he could fly private, he ran in a different social circle from me.

I worked to pay my rent. I had a nice enough apartment a couple of miles from here. A one bedroom on the sixteenth floor of the Sky House. But I didn't foresee ever having enough money to hop on a private jet to go anywhere.

I turned around in my chair and looked out the window. Watched all the cars going up and down the freeway.

I had to let him go. That was all there was to it. Even if there could have been the possibility of something between us, I wasn't going to find him.

He would merely be a memory. Like a summer romance. A fleeting love to remember fondly.

If nothing else, he had opened my eyes to realize that Franklin and I were not right for each other.

If there had ever been anything between me and Franklin, it wasn't there any longer and hadn't been for a very long time.

I turned back around in my chair. It was time for me to get some work done. I'd wasted enough time worrying about something I couldn't do anything about.

I blinked.

Christopher stood in the doorway.

37

CHRISTOPHER

'd had to make an appointment to get in to see Isla.

Her office was on the third floor of one of the medium sized buildings next to the 610 freeway.

I watched her for a few minutes until she saw me. I almost didn't recognize her. She was wearing a business shirt and jacket. Her hair was pulled back off her face.

And she was wearing shoes.

"Hi," I said, pushing off the door frame and stepping into the office. "You have a nice view."

"I do," she said, glancing over her shoulder as though to confirm that the view was still there.

"What are you doing here?" she asked.

"Finding you," I said, walking over to her desk. Not exactly the reception I had hoped for. But then I had caught her off guard.

I took it as a good sign that there was no ring on her finger.

"I didn't think I would see you again," she said.

"I felt like we left some things unsaid."

"That's true," she said, nodding. "Still...I'm a little surprised you found me."

"It wasn't that hard. I guess I had enough information."

"I didn't know how to find you," she said. "I didn't even know your last name."

"It's Worthington," I said, sitting in one of the two chairs across from her desk.

She sat back in her chair. Blinked at me.

"Worthington. As in Skye Travels?"

I shrugged. I didn't see any point in playing games. I'd already decided that she was the one I wanted.

There were a lot of times I kept my last name to myself, but this wasn't one of them. I was done with playing games.

She nodded slowly. "You called from there."

"I did. So… Franklin?"

"It wasn't working out," she said. "Didn't work out."

I wanted to ask more. To ask for details, but it didn't seem appropriate.

"Can I buy you lunch?" I asked.

She laughed.

"It's only nine o'clock in the morning."

"Brunch then," I said, then looked over my shoulder. "Or do you have to wait? I don't want to get you into trouble."

"I won't get into trouble. I'm not even supposed to be here this week."

"Why not?"

"The honeymoon," she said.

"Right. The honeymoon that didn't happen."

She locked her computer and slid her legal pad aside.

"Let's get out of here," she said, taking her purse from a desk drawer.

She didn't have to tell me twice.

After she locked her door, we walked past the receptionist's desk.

"I'm heading out, Trudy," she said. "I'll see you in the morning."

"You can take the day?" I asked as we waited for the elevator.

"I have some flextime," she said with a little shrug.

38

ISLA

emorial Park was starting to show signs of Fall. September in more northern parts of the country might mean leaf peeping season, but in Texas, it just meant that the morning heat was tolerate compared to the rest of the day.

The playground was deserted except for one child squealing with delight as his mother pushed him higher and higher in the swing.

"Reminds me of some good times with my brothers," Christopher said.

"I'd enjoy having some memories like that," I said. "Being an only child."

"Cousins?" he asked.

"Nope. Just me."

"I have boatloads of cousins around my age. Family get-togethers are chaos."

"I can't even imagine."

My head was still reeling with him being here. Not only that he had found me, but that he had gone to the trouble to find me. Had wanted to find me.

I felt surprised and honored and a little bit terrified.

I'd been thinking about him, even looked for him, even though it had been like looking for a needle in a haystack and I'd known going in that I wasn't going to find a man named Christopher in Houston with nothing else to go on.

I hadn't expected to find him. But he had found me. I wasn't sure what that meant. But I was cautious enough to know to be careful not to read too much into it.

"So," he said. "How are you?"

I kept my gaze on the path ahead. Debris from the storm littered the pathway. Limbs. Chunks of wood from park benches. The city had a lot of cleaning up and repairing to do.

It felt a little like my life. Debris littered after the storm that came after the disaster that was almost my wedding.

I had some cleaning up to do, too. And part of it was here, walking through the park with Christopher.

"I'm okay," I said. "Readjusting to being single again."

"Any word from Galveston? On how the house fared?" he asked, ignoring my statement.

"Not yet," I said, kicking a pinecone off the path.

"We can go see," I said. "When you're ready."

"I don't think they'll let anyone on the island."

"Probably not."

We walked in silence for a few minutes. A pair of red birds flew from a tree limb as we passed. Back to normal.

A jogger sped around us running ahead.

"It'll be too hot to be out here before long," I said, feeling a bit warm in my suit jacket.

"It's okay. We'll go get lunch."

I grinned over at him. He was so very handsome in his blue jeans and white USAF t-shirt and matching cap.

"Your grandfather is Noah Worthington?" I asked.

"Yes," he said.

Back to being a man of few words. He looked like just a

normal guy, walking around in his jeans and baseball cap. He did not look like the grandson of a multi-billionaire.

I nodded and stepped over a downed twig.

"Do you want to meet him?" he asked.

"What? I don't know."

"I met your family," he said. "It just seems fair."

I nodded. It did seem fair.

"Okay," I said.

It was very possible I was getting in over my head.

39

CHRISTOPHER

Today had been a good day. A really good day.

I'd found Isla. And she had been receptive to seeing me.

That had been an unknown when I set out on this venture to find her.

We sat at my grandparents' kitchen table. As it so often did, the scent of apple pie filled the air.

I was pretty sure that Grandpa and Grandma's live-in housekeeper/cook baked apple pies just to make the house smell good.

Even now, there was one in the oven.

Isla and I sat next to each other at the kitchen table. Grandpa sat across from us with a bottle of water in his hands.

"I hope you like apple pie," Grandpa said to Isla.

"I do," Isla said, with a glance at me. "Between the two of you, I'm going to starting taking my jogging more seriously."

Grandpa laughed. "This one likes to eat," he said, tilted his bottle toward me.

"Thanks," I said. "Nothing like family to point things out like they are."

"You met my family," she said.

"They're very good people," I told Grandpa.

"We'll invite them over," Grandpa said. "Get to know them."

Isla was looking a bit uncomfortable.

"We're going to walk outside. Sit by the fire pit and watch the lightning bugs," I said.

"Go ahead," Grandpa said. "Don't forget to come back. It would be a shame to make an old man eat fresh apple pie by himself."

"We'll be back," I said over my shoulder as I ushered Isla toward the door leading out to the courtyard.

"There's a fire pit?" she asked.

"Just give me a minute or two," I said. "I'll have it going."

"It's not cold."

"It's not about the heat," I said. "It's about the ambiance."

"Okay." She sat down on the bench and watched as I got a fire going in the pit.

"There," I said, sitting next to her on the bench.

"This is nice," she said. "I like your grandpa."

"Everyone does," I said. "His charm is part of what has made him so successful."

"It seems like charm is something that runs in the family."

"Thank you," I said. "For coming with me and meeting my grandpa. I've been talking about you for days."

"That's a little scary."

"It was all good."

"It's best if I don't know," she said. "Please don't tell me."

I held out a hand. "If I didn't like you, I wouldn't have looked you up."

"I know," she said.

When I held out a hand, she put hers in it and I clasped our fingers together.

"There's something I've been meaning to ask you."

"Okay," she said. "What is it?"

Her green eyes sparkled in the firelight as she looked at me curiously.

"I was wondering if I could kiss you again."

40

ISLA

By the time I got back to my apartment, I was walking on white puffy clouds.

We'd arranged for Christopher to pick me up tomorrow after work for us to see a movie.

"Hello Isla," Monica, the concierge at the Sky House said. "You have a package."

"Thank you," I said, stopping long enough to grab the little box. "This is Christopher," I said. "He'll be coming back tomorrow."

"Nice to meet you Christopher. I'll see you tomorrow."

Christopher walking me to my door involved going up the elevator and across the hall to my door.

"Do you want to—"

He put a finger gently on my lips, then kissed me. "I'll come in tomorrow," he said. "when I pick you up. That way it'll be like a first date."

"Okay," I said, a little amused by his gentlemanliness.

"Sweet dreams," he said.

He waited outside the door as I went inside and closed the door.

I flipped the lock and just stood there, giving my heart time to calm. I heard the elevator ding. Open and close. I pushed away from the door and went to look out the window.

When I'd gotten up this morning to go to work, I never would have thought that I would have ended the day with a goodnight kiss from Christopher.

I had been going to invite him in. Mostly just to be polite, I mused. But it was better this way. I liked the idea of having a first date with him tomorrow. I liked it a lot.

I was just heading to my bedroom when my doorbell rang.

Thinking it was Christopher, maybe changing his mind or maybe coming back for one more kiss, I threw open the door.

But it wasn't Christopher.

It was Franklin.

The blood drained from my face and the smile fell from my lips.

"Franklin," I said, surprised and a bit stunned. My head was full of Christopher and I hadn't given Franklin a thought in hours.

He pushed his way inside before I knew what he was up to. I left the door open.

"I think you owe me an explanation," he said, his words a bit slurred.

"Have you been drinking?" I asked, annoyed.

"Yes," he said. "I have. I've been drinking and thinking. I want my ring back."

"You can have it," I said, turning to go to the bedroom to get my… his ring.

He grabbed my arm. "We're supposed to be married now."

"Well, we're not," I said. "because you didn't show up."

"I have a bruise," he said, touching his cheek. The bruise was all but gone.

"You have to let me go if you want me to get your ring."

He swayed a bit and let me go.

I marched into my bedroom, opened my little wooden jewelry box where I'd stashed his ring until I figured out what to do about it.

When I turned around again, Franklin was standing at my bedroom door. I backed up and grabbed a little bottle of mace I kept on my nightstand. He didn't seem to notice that I was holding it behind my back.

"We need to reschedule," he said.

"Reschedule what?"

"The wedding."

I scoffed. "A wedding isn't something you can just reschedule."

"I insist," he said.

"The lady said no." It was Christopher. Christopher had come back and he was standing behind Franklin.

41

CHRISTOPHER

"Christopher," Monica, the concierge, called out to me as I passed by the desk.

I stopped, thinking she needed to scan my license or somehow otherwise put me on the list of people approved to visit Isla. I hoped the whole point of having a concierge was to keep the residents, Isla specifically, safe.

"I don't mean to get up in your business or anything," she said, keeping her voice low. But I think there's something you need to know."

"What is it?"

"Franklin, Isla's ex-fiancé just went upstairs. She took him off her list, but she must have forgotten he had a key fob. I tried calling her, but she didn't answer."

My whole system went into alert. My military training came back in one fell swoop.

"Push the access button," I said, taking off at a jog toward the bank of elevators.

I watched the numbers over the three elevators. Two going up. One coming down. I saw one stop at Isla's floor, then started down, seeming to move ever so slowly. Stopped at the third floor.

I shifted from one foot to the other. Seriously considering the stairs at this point.

Finally. The middle elevator made it to the lobby and the doors opened. I had to wait for a teenager struggling to handle three large dogs to step off the elevator.

"I'm sorry," she said, in response to what must have been my obvious impatience.

"No worries," I said, slipping past her onto the elevator. "Good luck."

I pushed the button to Isla's floor. Pushed it several times. Finally, the door slowly closed and the elevator started up.

I made it to her floor without any further incidents.

My blood ran cold as I saw her door standing open. Surely Franklin wouldn't hurt her. She'd been going to marry the man, for God' sake. But I also knew that didn't matter. He may have left her standing at the altar, but he may also feel jilted and that could cause people to do funny things.

Reaching the open door, I peeked inside. The first thing I noticed about the apartment was that it was small, opening into a kitchen. That and the scent of wildflowers. Fresh flowers maybe.

Following the sound of voices, I saw Franklin, his back to me, standing in a door to the right. Probably the bedroom.

"A wedding isn't something you can just reschedule," Isla said.

"I insist," Franklin said. I heard the alcohol in his voice, even in those two words. This would not do.

"The lady said no." I said, coming up behind him.

Franklin turned. "Who are you?" he asked.

Obviously he didn't remember me from the beach. Not that he would have had any reason to even notice me. He'd been there to get Isla and that had been it.

"I'm Christopher," I said. "Isla's friend."

"Friend, huh?" He put his hands on his waist. He was trying to look tough, but the effect was spoiled when he swayed a bit.

He looked over his shoulder at Isla. "Already making friends?"

Isla looked a bit like she was going to be sick.

"Just take your ring and go," she said. "Please." She stepped forward and held out the ring in her hand.

Franklin whirled around, slapping her hand away. The ring flew across the room, slamming into the floor-to-ceiling window.

The motion tipped her off balance and she fell to her knees.

I was normally an easy-going guy, but as Isla fell to the floor, I saw red.

I shoved past Franklin and went to her. He didn't concern me.

"Are you okay?" I asked her.

"I just lost my balance," she said, taking the hand that I held out for her. "I'm okay."

I had no more than gotten her to her feet and turned around when I saw a fist coming straight for me.

I blocked it with my arm, but then instinct kicked in.

It only took one blow for Franklin to be on the floor.

42

ISLA

When Franklin had shown up at my apartment door, I had still been in a haze from spending the day with Christopher.

I wasn't afraid of Franklin, exactly, but I was afraid of the situation. I knew that anyone, if pushed enough, could act erratically. And Franklin along with his present inebriated state was in a place to act erratically.

I didn't want his ring. I was only keeping it until I could figure how out to get it back to him.

I tried to hand him the ring, but when I did, all hell broke loose.

Somehow I was on the floor with Christopher helping me up.

I didn't see everything that happened next. But I did see Christopher slam his fist into Franklin's face.

Blood went everywhere, splashing over the quilt at the foot of my bed.

"You broke my nose," Franklin said, sitting up, both hands on his face.

"You shouldn't have come here," Christopher said. His tone

left no doubt whatsoever that Franklin would be leaving now. But then he held out his hand to help him up.

I scrambled to grab the ring from where it had landed on the floor. I pressed it into Christopher's hand as Franklin got his balance.

"Take this," Christopher said, passing the ring along.

"I don't want it," Franklin said.

"You're getting it anyway." Christopher dropped the ring into Franklin's shirt pocket. Then he physically escorted Franklin out the door, soundly closing it behind him.

Christopher turned and faced me.

"Thank you," I said, walking up to him and putting my arms around him. He was so strong and sturdy. And having him here left me feeling just plain safe.

"You can thank your friend downstairs."

"My friend?" I asked. "Monica?"

"She told me Franklin used his key fob."

"Right," I said. "I forgot he had that."

"They should be able to disable it."

I nodded and sat down on the sofa.

"Still…" I said, looking into his eyes as he sat next to me and took my hands in his.

"I need to talk to you about something."

"Okay." I wasn't sure how much more I could take. My emotions were all over the place right now.

"I was going to wait," he said. "to talk to you tomorrow on our date, but since I'm here I might as well go ahead."

A siren wailed on the freeway below and moonlight spilled into my little living room. My heart was pounding. Christopher had me on edge. The scented melted wax wasn't doing much to calm my nerves.

"I don't want to play games with you," he said. "I want to move forward. See if you take to me enough to make a go of this."

"Take to you?" I was having a hard time grasping what he was saying.

"Yes. To see if you like me enough."

"I like you," I said.

"Come here," he said, pulling me to him and cradling me against him, my head against his chest. He threaded his fingers into my hair.

"What do you mean by making a go?" I asked after a moment, pulling back to look up at him.

"I'm sure we can figure something out," he said, kissing me on the top of the head.

EPILOGUE

Isla

The airplane, a Seamax M-22, landed on the ocean in front of the West Beach near Galveston and the pilot deftly steered the airplane toward the beach.

It wasn't nearly as smooth as landing on the ground, but not nearly as bad as I had expected.

The sun was setting behind us, splashing the clear sky with an array of reds and golds. At the moment, both the sun and moon were visible in the clear evening sky.

As we floated toward the beach, I caught sight of the cottage.

"It looks okay from here," I said, leaning over to tell Christopher.

"I think it's okay," he said, seemingly unconcerned.

I narrowed my eyes at him.

"You already knew this, didn't you?"

He grinned. "I might have."

"You did." I elbowed him, but he just laughed.

"I wasn't about to let you come out here and get your heart broken."

I sighed.

In the two weeks since I had met Christopher here on this very beach we were currently headed toward, I had learned so much about him.

He was kind and caring and protective.

After docking on the beach, we went inside the quiet house. I saw nothing out of order. The hurricane must have simply brushed past it, doing no harm.

I wandered upstairs and that's where I found the letter, folded into a square, on the floor of my bedroom. It looked like it had just been randomly dropped. Maybe it fell out of a box or a handbag, but it sent a chill of my spine and a memory of that night long ago when I had seen Ophelia.

"What's that?" Christopher asked, coming up behind me.

When I didn't say anything, he reached down and picked up the letter. Handed it to me.

My hands trembled as I slowly unfolded it.

I immediately recognized the handwriting.

Dear Charles,

The storm is upon us and I fear that there may be no way out.

As I look out the window, I see waves coming in, spilling over the top of the house. It's beautiful and terrifying at the same time.

I don't know whether or not I'll make it out, but I want you to know that we're having a baby.

And I'll wait here for you. As long as it takes for you to come back, I'll wait.

Your loving wife,

Ophelia

"Oh my God," I said, leaning against Christopher.

I looked up at him. "Where did this come from?"

"I can't begin to imagine," he said.

"We were right," I said. "She was having a baby."

He nodded. "I guess she wanted us to know."

"I guess so."

The room was in shadows now.

"There's no electricity," I said, pointing out the obvious.

"Let's take a walk on the beach before it gets too dark," he said.

"Good idea. Will Bradford be okay?"

Bradford was our pilot. He wasn't with Skye Travels, but this whole experience had Noah Worthington thinking about buying a couple of seaplanes. It just made sense with Houston being this close to the beach.

"He'll be fine. Said he was going to walk down the coast a little. Find something to eat."

I took off my shoes as we reached the beach and let the damp sand squish through my toes as the waves tripped over my feet.

Christopher and I walked hand in hand down the beach about a half a mile before we turned around and started back.

"Do you think you could live here?" he asked.

"Maybe someday," I said. "My grandparents moved here after they retired."

"Your parents will probably do that, too."

"Probably," I said with a smile.

Moonbeams reflected over the ocean now, washing the house in an ethereal glow.

We slowed as we reached the house to leave the beach and start toward the house.

Christopher tugged my hand, stopping me.

"Look," he said, nodding toward the cottage.

"What?" Following his gaze, I looked up toward the second story window that I claimed as my room and Ophelia used as her room before.

There in the house, in the glow of a lantern somewhere behind them, stood Ophelia and a man that could only be Charles.

"How—"

There was no electricity in the house, but we could see them clearly.

Ophelia and Charles standing in an embrace. Charles holding an infant between them.

Ophelia looked up at him, a smile on her face.

"They're together," I said, hearing the wonder in my own voice.

"Together in eternity," he said. "Just as we will be."

And I knew he was right. I knew that if we were ever separated, I would wait for him through eternity. Time would cease to have any meaning.

And now instead of perpetually packing, Ophelia was content. She was with the man she loved.

I smiled up at Christopher, my eyes moist. He kissed me lightly on the lips.

Just as Ophelia had found her love, I had found mine.

Keep Reading for a Bonus Short Story, then a preview of
Unexpected Vows...

BESTSELLING AUTHOR

KATHRYN KALEIGH

WRITERS OF THE
FUTURE
HONORABLE
MENTION

Spells and other Useful Things

A SHORT STORY

Make sure to keep your doors locked. If anyone knocks on the door, do not answer it.

As I read the words, I heard some scuffling outside on the front porch.

Quietly, but quickly, dropping the open book onto the table, I dashed to the door and checked the lock. It was secure.

I turned, pressing my hands against my skirt. My heart was beating much too quickly.

It was nonsense, of course. A coincidence.

Peterson was sitting in the middle of the book, licking one of his hind legs.

Feeling a compulsion to preserve the book, nonsense though it may be, I grabbed Peterson up and cradling him on his back, held him close to me.

When someone knocked on the door, Peterson leaped out of my arms, skidding back onto the table. He went straight for his blanket, nudging his way beneath it, leaving only his tail showing.

"Some help you are," I said under my breath. There was still the matter of the person at the door.

If anyone knocks on the door, don't answer it.

1

———————

May 1863

The Yankees were coming.

Actually they were already here. I could hear them marching along the street outside my little two-story whitewashed cottage.

Everyone else - almost everyone else - had left for the caves.

With Vicksburg only an hour away from my little town of Le Tourneau, I was certain any accessible caves between here and there would be far too crowded for my taste.

I preferred to stay put.

I sat at the dining room table in the kitchen. The table was shoved against a window and I had the curtains pulled tight over it. I had one lit candle next to me, safely burning in a glass lantern.

I hoped the glow from the lantern was muted by the thick emerald velvet curtains. I preferred that the Yankees not come to my door. Like moths to a flame.

My long-haired cat, Peterson, sat in the middle of the dining room table. The cat was mostly white, but had splashes of gray here and there. He wore one of those splashes of gray like a mask on his face.

Peterson watched me as I turned the pages of an ancient over-sized book. The worn pages of the book were at least eighteen inches long. Though it was no more a quarter of an inch thick, it was by far the largest book I'd ever seen.

The brittle pages smelled like sulfur and though I probably should have found the scent to be distasteful, I actually found it to be intriguing.

Peterson narrowed his eyes at me and, though he'd been watching me in silence for about an hour, I could tell he was growing restless.

Peterson was about six months old. I'd found him in the barn after I'd just fed the horses. That was back when we had horses.

Peterson had walked right up to me, his tail held high and bunted my skirt. When the hoop skirt swayed back his way, he'd jumped back sideways in surprise. I'd laughed at him and he'd sat down, looking at me curiously.

I remembered the day well. There was actually a dusting of snow on the ground. That was something that never happened in this part of Mississippi.

Peterson had let me pick him up and carry him back to the house, cradling him on his back. I'd immediately fallen in love with his soft kitten fur.

I'd set him right here on this dining room table and ever since then, he'd acted like the table was his personal space.

So I'd put him a blanket on the table and he'd learned to nuzzle his way beneath it. Sometimes on those cold winter days, if he couldn't manage to get himself covered up, he'd meow until I came over and helped him out. He'd spend hours sleeping under that blanket.

But now that it was warmer, he'd just sit on top of the

blanket and nap. Or watch me. Whichever he found to be more interesting at the time.

Since Father was off fighting for the cause and Mother, as far as I knew - which wasn't too far - had gone with him, I was left in the house by myself.

I wasn't supposed to be here, but that was another story.

On a cold rainy day in March, Peterson and I had gone exploring in the attic. I'd been a little nervous about the rickety ladder that we had to climb to get through the little attic door, but Peterson had jumped up there like it was nothing.

There were mostly just old paintings and boxes of clothes that no one wanted any more. There was a trunk full of letters that I might look through one day, but right now, with everything going on with the war, they didn't interest me so much. There was also an old clock and a several lanterns.

Somehow someone had put an old rocking chair up there, though I have no idea how they'd lifted it up those attic stairs and managed to get it through the door that was only about four or five feet square.

Probably Grandfather. He could do just about anything.

Grandfather had died ten years ago when I was nine years old. He'd taught me most of what I knew.

When I was growing up, Mother spent most of her days sewing for those people who could afford to buy fancy ball gowns and Father spent his time working in a sawmill near Jackson. Jackson was far enough away that Father had to live with a bunch of other men in a bunker. So we rarely saw Father, though he occasionally stopped by and gave Mother money.

Grandpa never said much about Father, but he always got a funny look on his face when Father showed up.

On those days, Grandpa would take me fishing or out riding horses. Always keeping me away from the house when Father was home.

I never asked him why and frankly, never gave it much thought at the time.

After all, he was the one I spent my days with anyway.

But he never showed me this book.

Spells and Other Useful Things.

Not a very creative title for a book, but quite descriptive for what seemed to be just that. Spells and so far other things like recipes.

I was only about two pages into the book, having just turned one of the large brittle pages, when Peterson stepped over and laid down on top of the open book.

"What is it, Peterson?" I asked. "Are you hungry?"

I went to the pantry and crumbled up some dried chicken on a saucer. Usually, Peterson would have already been on the floor, rubbing against my skirts by the time I had his saucer out, but right now, he just stretched onto his back and rolled against the brittle pages.

"Come on, Peterson." Since I had just found the book and still didn't know what kind of significance it might hold, I didn't want the wayward kitten to destroy it.

So I picked Peterson up and placed him on the floor next to his saucer.

He started eating like he was supposed to.

I sighed and went back to sit at the table.

Two soldiers passed by outside my window, talking loudly. My window was about ten, maybe fifteen, feet away from the street. I couldn't understand what the soldiers were talking about, but a few words were discernible.

Siege. Vicksburg. Cigars.

I could tell they were Yankees by their accent.

I probably should have been afraid of them, but I wasn't.

Peterson finished his chicken and jumped back onto the table.

With a fake stern look, I moved the book out of his way,

holding it up instead. I shifted it toward the soft glow of the candle so I could see the faint ink on the pages a little better.

There at the top of page three were the words *What to do in the event of a siege.*

I angled the book closer to the light, certain I'd read it wrong.

Beneath the title was a list of five things.

The first item read *Keep your light dim. Preferably away from any windows.*

I glanced at the thick curtains. Depending on whether or not there was a full moon - I didn't even know what the moon looked like tonight - my candle may or may not be visible from outside through the window.

I moved the candle further away from the window just in case. Peterson licked his paws as though he'd just remembered to wash up after eating his chicken.

I moved to the second item on the list.

Make sure to keep your doors locked. If anyone knocks on the door, do not answer it.

As I read the words, I heard some scuffling outside on the front porch.

Quietly, but quickly, dropping the open book onto the table, I dashed to the door and checked the lock. It was secure.

I turned, pressing my hands against my skirt. My heart was beating much too quickly.

It was nonsense, of course. A coincidence.

Peterson was sitting in the middle of the book, licking one of his hind legs.

Feeling a compulsion to preserve the book, nonsense though it may be, I grabbed Peterson up and cradling him on his back, held him close to me.

When someone knocked on the door, Peterson leaped out of my arms, skidding back onto the table. He went straight for his blanket, nudging his way beneath it, leaving only his tail showing.

"Some help you are," I said under my breath. There was still the matter of the person at the door.

If anyone knocks on the door, don't answer it.

It was an old, ancient book, its pages faded and tattered. What could the words possibly have to do with right now?

But instead of going to the door, I went back to my chair at the table and the list of things to do in the event of a siege.

It didn't even say what kind of siege.

I went to number three.

Number three. *Find a good hiding place.*

I had to put a hand over my mouth to keep from laughing out loud.

Peterson had this one figured out already.

I looked around. There was no place to hide in here. Maybe I should go back to the attic. But I wasn't leaving Peterson here and I had a feeling there was no way I was going to get him into the attic.

I turned my attention back to the book. Perhaps I needed to know what was next before I abandoned the book for a hiding place.

Number Four. *Create a spell.*

The rest of number four and number five were smeared from Peterson's licking.

Create a spell?

What kind of spell? And then what?

The man knocked again. I could tell it was a man just by the way he knocked.

A soldier.

I tossed the blanket over Peterson's tail and blew out the candle.

The book's words seemed sound. And I saw no reason not to follow them.

Peterson made a sound. I couldn't tell if it was a protest or a thank you.

I closed the book and left it to go toward the stairs. There were two bedrooms upstairs and surely I could find a hiding place up there.

I lifted my skirts and was just about to put a foot on the bottom step when the man on the other side of the front door said my name.

"Miss Charlotte?"

I froze, since my name was indeed Charlotte.

I tried to think who might know I was here, but I couldn't come up with anyone.

Nonetheless, I had grown up here, so there were any number of people who could have known me before I left home after my grandfather died.

"Charlotte? Are you in there?"

I didn't recognize the voice.

And he didn't sound like a Yankee after all. Not that I had ever personally spoken to a Yankee. I'd merely heard snatches of their conversations as they passed by on the street.

Peterson was watching me now, peeking out from beneath the blanket. I could just see the glow of his eyes.

Squinting his eyes, his reached out and slapped the book to the floor with one paw.

So much for being quiet and not letting the man know I was in here.

The book had fallen open and I gently picked it up, placing it on the table. Why was Peterson being so difficult?

The cat swished his tail against the window, allowing the glow of a moonbeam to splash across the open book.

Number Five. *If the man knows your name, you must let him inside.*

I stared at the words. Read through the list again. Keep down the light. Lock the door. Hide. *Cast a spell.* Let him inside.

My eyes narrowed, I looked up at Peterson. He was resting his face on his paws, looking quite innocent, at least for a cat. If a cat could look innocent.

I was beginning to think that cats were not innocent creatures at all.

"What do you want me to do Peterson?" I asked in a whisper. Here I was. Looking to ancient books and cats for answers to a real world problem.

What had the world come to?

Peterson flipped his tail and the room was in darkness again.

I heard the sound of soldiers marching this way. Soldiers marching by moonlight.

I didn't even have time to process the question of soldiers marching at night, when the knocking started again. Frantic now.

"Charlotte. Please. Let me in."

The man not only knew me. He knew I was in here. And he sounded like he was in danger.

"The Yankees are coming."

I heard it then. The fear in his voice.

Cats and book be damned.

I threw open the lock and a man, who must have been leaning hard against it, fell onto the floor. In my foyer.

But before I had time to process it all, he was back on his feet. He closed the door and slammed the lock home.

"Come on," he said, taking my hand and leading me up the stairs.

I couldn't even see the stairs, but he seemed to have no problem seeing in the dark and besides that, he knew exactly which way to go.

I bunched up my skirts with my free hand. I had no choice, really, but to go with him. My feet barely seemed to touch the ground as he pulled me along behind him.

When we reached the top of the stairs, I realized that all the curtains were open on the second floor and moonlight streamed in through the open windows. I rarely went up here. The house seemed much more manageable if I just ignored the fact that there was a second floor.

He turned right, towards what used to be my bedroom. In another lifetime.

Peterson dashed past us, running into the bedroom just ahead of us.

How was it that a cat who'd been hiding beneath a blanket just a few seconds ago, could now be darting ahead of us? Just like this soldier who obviously knew my house as well as I did, Peterson seemed to be heading the same place we were.

Just as he closed the bedroom door behind the three of us, I heard the Yankees pounding against the door. Then I heard the distinct sound of wood splintering. The Yankees were inside the house.

Whoever wrote the book of spells and useful things had gotten the order wrong. It should have been open the door, then hide. Or just hide.

"Now what?" I asked out loud, mostly to myself.

The man shoved the armoire aside. It was a large armoire that was nearly as tall as the ceiling. And heavy. I'd never known it to be moved. Not even during the annual Spring cleaning ordeal. He pressed on wall, up high, and the wall opened up.

Then we were through the wall - that was actually a door - and began shoving the armoire back in place.

"Wait," I said, putting a hand on his upper arm. "My cat."

The man nodded over his shoulder. I followed his gaze.

Peterson had slipped into the secret room and sat behind me, his eyes narrowed.

Using the little bit of moonlight that streamed in through

the bedroom window, the man lit a candle and using the dim light, put the wall back together.

As my heart rate slowed a little, I saw that the room was small. Only about six feet by four feet. No windows.

But there was a box full of candles and some jars of dried fruit.

What was this place? In my own home, there was a room I didn't know about.

As my gaze was drawn back to the stranger who knew my name, he put a finger to his lips, cautioning me to stay quiet.

Footsteps echoed as the enemy soldiers wandered the house. It would be obvious to anyone that someone was recently home. The candle at the dining room table would still be warm if anyone bothered to check.

There would still be crumbs of chicken in Peterson's food saucer. He always left crumbs when he ate.

I held my breath as soldiers walked through my bedroom, then I exhaled slowly as they left the upper floor.

The strength left my limbs and I leaned against the wall. Peterson jumped up on the one small table in the room and head bunted me. It was just like him to make himself at home on the only table in the room.

In the dim candlelight, I studied the soldier then. He was watching me as well.

He was a young man, perhaps somewhere around my age. His hair was too long. It fell against his collar. And he needed a shave. So I couldn't tell much about what he looked like.

But his eyes were kind.

"Who are you?" I asked in a whisper.

"I'm Peter." He was surprised I didn't know who he was, but he hid it well.

I looked over at my cat. "This is Peterson."

"You named your cat after me?"

"What?" I straightened. This was all much too surreal. The book. The soldiers. The secret room.

Now a savior with almost the same name as my cat.

"Charlotte," he said, his voice kind. "You don't remember me. But it was a long time ago."

"Should I?" I asked. "Remember you?"

"I knew you before you left. I knew your grandfather."

"But how?"

He slipped off his cap and tucked it into his pants pocket. "I worked in the stables. My family had a farm just down the road."

Realization hit me slowly. Like a slow ocean wave heading toward me that seemed to take forever to get there, but nearly knocked me down when it hit.

"Peter." I remembered the boy in the stables. He'd been a couple of years younger than I was and I could always tell that Grandfather had a fondness for him.

I knew that sometimes Grandfather worked with him in the stables and took him fishing and such when I was studying or doing needlepoint or reluctantly practicing the piano.

I'd asked Grandfather about him a few times, but Grandfather always just shrugged off an answer. "He's just a boy from down the road. He doesn't have anyone, so I try to teach him a few things."

But I'd known. I'd known that Grandfather had a fondness for him that was different than what he felt for me. Grandfather had no sons and no grandsons. No one to pass along the things that a man would naturally teach a boy.

Grandfather had taught me to ride, too. I could ride as well as any boy and I could even shoot a gun. But I also had to learn things he couldn't teach me. Like needlepoint and piano. He wanted me to be accomplished. I knew he was proud of me. I hadn't been jealous of Peter. Just curious as any child would be, but not enough to worry about it.

"What's this room?" I asked, needing to pull my thoughts away from my Grandfather.

He looked a bit sheepish. "When I realized the war was going to happen, I built it. As a safe place for anyone who might need it."

"You knew I was coming back."

"I knew that you might. I knew that you'd be out of school. And that was enough for me."

Peterson nudged at my hand until I petted him on the head. "You built this room for me." It was more of a statement than a question.

"It was the least I could do."

I picked up Peterson and cradled him to me. "What do you mean?"

"Your grandfather left this house to me." He cleared his throat. "Sort of. He told me to promise to keep it for you. If you ever wanted to live here again, I was to help you. If you didn't want it, I could live here." He shrugged. "Then there was the war, so I had to go."

"Of course." He had to go fight. It was his duty.

I was trying to remember Peter. I hadn't paid him a whole lot of attention. He was just a boy. And well, boys hadn't held much interest to me back when I was a child.

"Look," he said. "I'm sorry I frightened you. But I need to take care of something. But..." he paused. "I really don't want to lock you in here."

He was looking at me with an odd expression, his eyes bright, a little smile playing about his lips.

"I don't really want to be locked in here."

"I'll leave the armoire moved and leave it so that you can close yourself up in here. If you need to."

I nodded. I was still trying to wrap my head around this soldier, Peter, being the same little boy who'd followed my grandfather around in the barn, learning about horses and such.

He smiled at me, then gently took my hand and kissed the back of it.

My face felt a little flushed. Peter certainly wasn't a child now.

He moved the wall, then shoved the armoire aside, and with a quick nod, left me standing there, holding Peterson.

2

———————

Three weeks later

I sat at the little dining room table. The curtains were wide open, letting the warm sunshine in.

Peterson lay in the sunshine, stretched out on his back, his stomach full from his dinner of dried chicken and fresh biscuits I'd made just that morning.

The Yankees had passed through our little town, moving on uneventfully. Vicksburg, it seemed, was of much greater importance for whatever their purpose was than Le Tourneau.

I hadn't spent any more time in the secret room that Peter had built, but I'd used the candles and I'd eaten some of the dried fruit.

I was sitting at the table peeling some potatoes to make some soup for later. I had the book, *Spells and Other Useful Things*, open on the table in front of me. There was a recipe for soup and I just happened to have everything I needed.

I'd been thinking about my options for things I could do after the war was over.

One thing I was considering was taking up my mother's

work as a seamstress. Once the war was over, people were going to need clothing. Especially dresses.

In fact, I had a piece of paper on the table and had written down some things I'd need to buy before I started offering my services. Likes needles and pins.

A movement outside the window caught my attention.

There was a soldier walking toward the front door. I watched as he came up the porch stairs then lost sight of him as he reached the door.

Although he looked different - clean-shaven and his hair was short - I knew it was Peter.

My heart pounded in my chest as I got up to answer the door.

I tucked my hair behind my ears, then pulled it to one side. I was wearing an old faded yellow dress that had seen better days.

I took a deep breath and opened the door. My hands were shaking.

I didn't remember anything much about Peter as a child, but I'd certainly been thinking about him a lot for the last three weeks.

There was so much I wanted to know. I wanted to know how he'd kept up with me... and more importantly, why.

Oh my. In the bright sunshine, I could see the bright blue of his eyes. Now that he'd shaven, I could see what I couldn't tell before.

Peter was a handsome man.

So very handsome. With clear skin and warm kissable lips.

"Come in," I said, backing up to give him space to come inside. "I'm just in the kitchen making some soup."

He followed me inside. "How are you?" he asked as we walked into the kitchen.

Peterson was sitting in the middle of the table, his eyes bright, his ears forward.

"Good," I said, with a smile over my shoulder. "Sit. I'll make you some coffee."

Peter sat down at the table in my chair. I set the kettle on the stovetop.

"Have you been writing?" he asked.

"Yes," I said, taking two mugs from the cabinet.

I turned back and saw him looking at the open book, *Spells and Other Useful Things*.

The paper I'd been writing on was underneath the table.

Peterson was looking at me with a smug expression. Then he lifted a paw and licked it delicately.

"This is an interesting poem," Peter said, turning in the chair, a devilish grin on his face.

"What?" I took a step forward. "The soup recipe?"

He lifted an eyebrow. "Looks like a poem to me."

Reading over Peter's shoulder, I realized the poor man knew absolutely nothing about poetry.

There were lines on the page opposite the soup recipe, but any rhyming was questionable.

During a bright flower moon,

I met a man named Peter.

Peter set my heart aflutter.

And if ever I see Peter again,

I think I shall marry him.

I stepped back with a gasp. "I didn't write..."

Peter was grinning from ear to ear.

I looked over at Peterson. The cat finished licking his other paw and blinked innocently, swishing his tail with satisfaction.

Keep Reading for a Preview of Unexpected Vows...

PREVIEW UNEXPECTED VOWS

Chapter 1
Emma Blake

Today was going to be a good day.

April weather in Houston was stunningly beautiful. It was still winter in a lot of the country and all of Canada. Take Vancouver, for instance. Today was rainy with a high of thirty-five degrees.

I parked in my assigned spot in the second floor of the garage, grabbed my oversized tote bag and Starbuck's latte, and took the elevator down to the ground floor. I was early, as always, so I was the only one on the elevator. I liked it that way. It was one of the many ways that I avoided small talk.

The door opened and I stepped out, my red-bottomed heels tapping on the concrete. The shoes pinched my feet and scraped the backs of my ankles, but image was everything. Tonight I would reward myself with a hot bath and soak away the soreness. Then tomorrow I would do it all over again.

I could have turned left and walked inside, using the staff elevator to get to my office. Instead, I turned right toward the visitor's entrance. Using the sidewalk allowed me to soak up a few minutes of sunshine before I spent the rest of the day tucked away in my air-conditioned office. Two butterflies flitted around the row of pink and white daisies lining the walkway while a bluebird did a touch and go over one of the half dozen wooden benches.

The usual food truck called *Morning and Noon* sat in its usual place in the parking lot. They had THE best egg and cheese biscuits and lattes that were as good as the one in my hand. Although there was no line yet, I didn't stop. Not having to get my own breakfast or lunch was one of the perks of being a Senior Architect.

"Good morning, Miss Blake," Bob, the doorman said as he opened the door for me.

"Good morning, Bob. Is Harrison here yet?"

I already knew that he wasn't, but I liked Bob. He was a good man.

"No ma'am. Not yet. He'll be here though."

"Uh huh." I slid my shades up to the top of my head and walked inside. "I know." The receptionist, Misty, liked those scented humidifiers, so the lobby always smelled like cinnamon or vanilla and spruce trees during December.

"Have a good day," Bob said.

"You too, Bob."

I pushed the button to go up to the tenth floor. My employer, Skye Designs, occupied floors ten and eleven. There was only one more floor above that—the Skye Travels corporate office. They were the least busy since their main office was at the airport. A waste of good space, but no one asked me.

One of my associates had designed a rooftop work and lounge area and was waiting on board approval. I'd seen the plans and was looking forward to having the outdoor space to use as a place to take a break from my desk. Taking a cue from Las Vegas, he was proposing using an outdoor misting system. With the Houston weather as hot as it was during the long summer months, those misting systems were becoming more and more popular. In fact, I was proposing private patio misting systems as part of my current project design.

Stepping off the elevator, I walked down the hallway to my corner office and dropped my tote bag on my desk. Taking my coffee, I went to the window and looked out over the Uptown Galleria area. This building was on the western edge of River Oaks, giving me a south and west view.

I'd lived in New York for all of eleven months before being recruited to Houston by Skye Designs. I'd established a good reputation based partly on my motto "Less is More." One of the Worthington Enterprises board members, a woman named Ainsley Beaufort, had purchased one of the New York condos based on my designs. She'd liked it so much, she'd offered me a job at her company in Houston.

It was hard to turn down a position as senior architect, especially with the salary they offered. But it wasn't New York, something I was still on the fence about.

A police car pulled up to front of the building and parking. I shrugged. Not my business.

Wanting to get some creative work done before my meetings started, I sat at my drafting desk and did some sketches.

Chapter 2
Harrison Moore

GRABBING two egg and cheese biscuits and two lattes from the food truck outside the office, I glanced at my watch. I was still early enough.

As an executive assistant, if I wasn't early to work, I was late. And I had to come with breakfast in hand or there would be hell to pay.

"Good morning, Bob," I said as I hurried through the door he held open.

"Boss is upstairs." Bob's voice held a note of warning.

"I had no doubt," I said over my shoulder, heading toward the elevators.

I punched the button with my elbow and took a taste of my coffee. Not bad. I usually preferred my coffee cold, but it easier to just order two hot coffees.

Getting on the elevator, I punched eleven with my elbow and nearly spilled coffee.

I squared my shoulders and waited for the doors to open.

The tenth floor, like the rest of the two-year-old building was plush and understated. Worthington Enterprises was expanding so quickly and in so many different directions, they had decided to form a corporation and build their own building to house the myriad divisions they were developing.

The top floor was occupied by Skye Travels. The legendary founder of the Skye Travels airline company, Noah Worthington, still came into the office on occasion. And even though it was only on occasion, he had the best office in the building.

A perk of being the founder.

The tenth and eleventh floors belonged to Skye Designs. Founded by one of Noah's daughters, it was one of the newest and fastest growing architectural firms in the country. Texas was perfect for the Worthingtons. Go big or go home could be their motto.

That was one reason why I chose to work here. Another thing the Worthingtons believed in was starting from the ground up. Unless, of course, a person was like Emma Blake who brought their reputation with them.

If you start at the bottom, you know how things run from the inside out, Noah had told me on the day he'd hired me as an executive assistant.

I dropped off one coffee and one biscuit at my desk and knocked on Emma's door.

"Come," she said.

I rolled my eyes. Would it seriously hurt her to say *come in* instead of *come?*

"Good morning, Miss Emma," I said.

She didn't bother to glance up from her protractor.

"Breakfast is on your table," I said as I set the coffee and biscuit on the little table next to one of the floor-to-ceiling windows. Why she didn't work there, I didn't know. If this were ever my office, I'd put my drafting table right in front of this window.

I shrugged when she didn't respond and walked back out.

"Thank you," she said, just before I closed the door behind me.

Emma wasn't all that bad. She expected five hundred percent from everyone, including herself. Always first to arrive in the mornings and last to leave at night, she had no social life. In the four months I'd worked for her, I'd never once recorded a social engagement on her calendar. No personal phone calls. Nothing. Just work. Notwithstanding her hairstylist, personal trainer and nutritionist.

The oddest part about her lack of a social life was that she was a looker. Five four, one hundred twenty pounds, long brunette hair secured at the back of her head with a clip. A heart-shaped face with emerald green eyes and perfectly bow-shaped lips.

Always dressed professionally, I'd never seen her without a suit jacket. And heels. The woman always wore heels.

Sitting at my own desk I ate my breakfast while I checked messages and reviewed her calendar.

Maybe, just maybe, I'd have a few minutes to work on my own project today while she was in a meeting.

Just as I was caught up, a message popped up on my screen.

EMMA: *I need you in my meeting this morning.*

So much for that. I didn't know how I was supposed to ever be successful with my own project if I was always running after Emma Blake.

Chapter 3
Emma

MY ASSISTANT, Harrison Moore, sat next to me with his iPad open and ready to take notes while we waited for Mr. Jackson Fleming.

Mr. Fleming had a large corner office on the eleventh floor with a perfect view of downtown Houston. He had this office in Houston and one at the airport. He wasn't an architect. He was a pilot.

But he and his wife had founded Skye Designs, so there was no one to complain to about how the office could be better used by someone who worked there every day. Besides, he was the head of Skye Designs.

I used the wait time to check my emails.

"Did you follow up on this question from Robert Johnson?"

"Yes ma'am," Harrison said.

Harrison had been my assistant since I'd gotten here. I hadn't picked him and hadn't asked questions. Whoever picked him had made a good choice.

What I did know was that he was my age and had an

architectural degree from the University of Houston. Though it wasn't part of my job description, I planned to begin mentoring him after I got a handle on my own projects.

I also knew that he was far too handsome with deep blue eyes that always seemed to hold a secret smile. By the end of the day he had a five o'clock shadow that added a bad boy sheen to his boy next door looks.

Not that I noticed. He was my assistant. And work was not a dating pool.

With nothing of interest in my email, I locked the phone and tapped a finger against the screen.

"Do you know what this meeting is about?" I asked.

"No ma'am," he said, with a glance in my direction. "You don't?"

"Nuh-uh."

Finally, Mr. Fleming walked in and sat at his desk.

He was always a pleasant man, but at the moment he was wearing a scowl.

I braced myself, for what, I didn't know.

"I've been on the phone all morning," he said, without preamble.

"Is something wrong with the Martin account?" I'd been working on the Martin account since I got here four months ago.

It was a planned mid-rise condominium unit near the Highland shopping center in River Oaks. A labor of love for me. Everything I believed in. *Less is more.* Comfortable housing, designed especially for those who worked from home. No gold faucets that were prohibitive to using. Just high quality and clean lines.

"I'm afraid I have some bad news."

Why hadn't Mr. Martin come to me? If there was a problem with the designs, he should have come to me.

"I can fix it," I said. "He should have come to me."

"It isn't Mr. Martin's account."

I glanced over at Harrison. He shook his head almost imperceptibly.

I forced a smile that I was certain looked fake.

"I don't understand—"

"You're being deported," Mr. Fleming said.

"What? Why? I don't—"

"Your Visa expired."

"No," I said. "I renewed it. I have a letter. The paperwork is in progress."

"I'm sorry," he said. "It was denied."

I inhaled deeply. I could still fix this.

"Okay," I said. "I'll just go to Vancouver for six months. Work remotely. I can reapply and come right back."

Mr. Fleming was shaking his head.

"I already proposed that. They said no."

"You don't know how this…" I said. "I'll go to the Immigration office. Straighten it all out."

"Emma," he said. "This is serious. I bought you twelve hours. They were coming to arrest you."

A knot formed in the pit of my stomach. I'd seen the police car myself. I put a hand to my waist to brace myself.

"Arrest? But… I…" I didn't do anything wrong. I went to work every day. I worked hard.

I hadn't set foot in Canada since the day I'd left for college. Going back to Vancouver wasn't an option. My architectural license was here. In the states.

"I agreed to put you on a flight to Vancouver and fly you there myself."

"They can't do that," Harrison said, speaking up suddenly.

I looked at Harrison. I didn't even think he liked me all that much, but here he was going to bat for me.

Keep Reading Unexpected Vows…

Kathryn Kaleigh writes sweet contemporary romance, time travel romance, and historical romance.

kathrynkaleigh.com

www.ingramcontent.com/pod-product-compliance
Lightning Source LLC
Chambersburg PA
CBHW030431120726
47903CB00003B/912